AND BITTER WIND

A NOVEL OF THE CALIFORNIA GOLD FIELDS

EARL MURRAY

A TOM DOHERTY ASSOCIATES BOOK
NEW YORK

BLOOD AND BITTER WIND: A NOVEL OF THE CALIFORNIA GOLD FIELDS

A Forge Book
Published by Tom Doherty Associates, LLC
175 Fifth Avenue
New York, NY 10010

www.tor.com

Forge® is a registered trademark of Tom Doherty Associates, LLC.

ISBN 0-812-57517-2
EAN 978-0812-57517-2

First edition: August 2004
First mass market edition: August 2004

Printed in the United States of America

0 9 8 7 6 5 4 3 2 1

FOR ABEL GANDARA
AND JENNIFER CAMPBELL-GANDARA

THANKS FOR YOUR MUCH APPRECIATED
FRIENDSHIP.

ACKNOWLEDGMENTS

A vast number of volumes, essays, and articles have been written about the California Gold Rush and its effect on California society, much of it indispensable to me in the creation of this work. Many diaries and journals have also been published that gave me a clear, firsthand view of the people who traveled to and lived in the mining camps. I would like to acknowledge them all and each individual who took the time to research their work and see it into print.

I would especially like to acknowledge the stories and information provided me by my good friend Joel Torres and his family, whose ancestors knew the celebrated bandido, Joaquín Murrieta. The oral histories of both the man and the times were invaluable in my research efforts.

BLOOD
AND
BITTER WIND

ONE

The storm surged in from nowhere, turning the calm seas into enormous, white-capped swells. At the tempest's mercy, the steamer *Rosa Maria* rose and fell and turned in every direction, while her passengers screamed into the raging wind.

John Dimas held fast to an iron ladder that led to the second level. He struggled to keep his grip, determined to avoid the turmoil on the deck below. The seas churned beneath the steamer and already men lay groaning and dying from the impact of heavy cargo that slammed against their bodies.

Yells and screams rose from below, from cabins and quarters filled with trapped passengers, a hundred and fifty terrified souls. Dimas watched as a woman holding a small child emerged and was hauled back, shrieking, by a large man in a dark suit.

A red dawn bodes no good, he had heard often

enough. Had he the opportunity again, he would have paid closer attention to that small voice that had spoken from within himself that very morning. He might have insisted they allow him a boat to row himself toward the California shoreline. Certainly not advisable, but preferable to the present situation.

They had been within a half-day's journey to San Pedro's port, just a half day to the beginning of his personal quest, and the crew had all agreed that surely there could be no troubled seas before the sun hit the zenith for the day. So he had gone along with them, believing their assessment to be accurate, even though the pit of his stomach remained knotted. "Always listen to that part of you," his mother had advised many times.

She carried the blood of three different races in her veins, and the collective wisdom of all those elders. "That is where your soul lives, and your soul will never deceive you," she had instructed. "All manner of men can speak in any tongue or voice, but that part of you will always understand where danger lies and where calm mornings can be found. Remember that."

Dimas, along with the others, had awakened to a calm morning with a blood-red sky, and it seemed they might beat the storm to port after all. Everyone felt anxious to get on from San Pedro to El Pueblo de la Reina de los Angeles, the Town of the Queen of

Angels, and begin the trip toward instant wealth. The foothills along the lower Sierra Nevada, the southern mines, as they were called, were now regarded as a destination well worth pursuing. Tent towns had filled the gulches and miners were crowding every stream. Seemingly, another gold camp emerged almost daily. Someone would announce a new strike and, light or dark, many if not everyone would leave immediately for the new diggings.

Dimas was not a crowd follower, though, and was not in search of wealth. Instead, his search was of another nature, much more demanding and with no real reward, except that it might clear his conscience and allow his dearly departed mother to rest in peace.

He had no intention of announcing his mission to anyone, at least not right away. There would be those who would side with him and those who would become sudden, and likely dangerous, enemies. For the time being he would embark on his quest alone and take what chances necessary to accomplish it. If he discovered gold along the way, then so much the better.

As noon approached, he had kept his mind on the thought of getting where he wanted to go early and with success. The morning had passed quickly, and everyone began feeling the excitement of reaching port.

Everything had changed, though, with sudden engine trouble. The vessel had drifted out farther to sea while the crew worked with fever to repair the problem. Meanwhile, the skies had darkened and the wind had changed and the sea birds had all abandoned the area. Dimas had known the fate of the vessel even as the engine trouble had been repaired when a number of rats had jumped onto the starboard railing, squeaking to one another.

At that point, he had secured his .44 Colt pistol and his Bowie knife tightly to his waist, winding cord around and around the weapons, and then looping it around his belt. Though he had never before been in a sea storm, the part of him where his soul dwelled spoke clearly that he would soon learn what the worst of them could produce and that under no circumstances, when it was finished, should he be without something for defense.

Now, sodden with a deluge of rain, trapped in a darkness streaked overhead with giant bolts of lightning, Dimas and the other passengers faced death in the form of monstrous walls of water. No escaping it. Nowhere to find refuge. Only the flimsy ladder kept him from the raging sea. But it had already begun tearing itself away from the side as he held fast against the force of the wind. In but little time either he would be blown loose, or should he maintain the strength to keep a grip, the ladder and he, both, would fly off into the thrashing torrent.

Dimas realized that the journey had been vexed from the beginning. No one had spoken anything but a few words to him the entire trip down from San Francisco, in effect telling him they were all headed in a direction that didn't include him. Call it a superstition, but it was very real to him, a plain sign he had learned to look for during his life of thirty-three years. Before battle, especially, men seemed to know when their last earthly days approached. The blood and dust of the Mexican War in Texas hadn't yet settled from his mind.

He squinted in the rain, its force stinging him like embers. His back and arms ached. As the storm worsened and the ship moaned and began to break apart, the lower deck suddenly filled with frantic passengers bursting up from below. Their screams and cries escalated as the sea surged over the leeward side, foaming and smashing, lifting flailing bodies onto its back. As the waves receded, rolling bodies vanished into the raging torrent.

The wind tore at the vessel without mercy, ripping and popping with the sound of a large whip. Just above Dimas, the stack creaked and leaned toward him, ready to topple with the next heavy blast. An intense flash of lightning revealed a cliff that rose into the night, and rocks just off the starboard bow.

Dimas prepared himself for the grating, grinding jolt that followed as the steamer piled into the rocks.

The bow reared up and the stack broke free. It tore past his right side on its destructive fall into the throng of passengers just below, stripping rails and planks and bodies as it careened off into the churning sea. The storm then pulled the ship back from the rocks, as if it were a toy in a bathtub, throwing more cargo and people and wreckage over the side.

In resignation the *Rosa Maria* tipped to leeward. A sailor who had made it to Dimas's position crashed over the top of him, clutching desperately at the ladder. His left hand found a grip just below Dimas's feet and their combined weight ripped the last remaining bolts free. "God have mercy on me!" the sailor screamed, and dropped into the swirling foam.

As the ladder gave way, Dimas wrapped his arms and legs around a loose plank and suddenly found himself beneath a wave. Water and darkness, cold to the bone. He gasped as the wave spit him up into the air. He released the plank and reached out for something larger, more buoyant, that rose in front of him. He latched onto a huge trunk, twisting a loose leather strap around his right wrist and arm. He didn't care that his arm might be wrested from the shoulder socket and torn loose. It wouldn't matter, for should that occur, he would be lost anyway.

In the darkness and the madness, Dimas lost all hold on conscious thought. He fell into that narrow lane of existence between life and death—that channel of desperation well past the last edge of endurance, where letting go would be far easier than running the course. The temptation to allow it to engulf him was strong—far stronger and much farther into the decision than his bullet wounds had taken him during the war. It could all be over in the blink of an eye, a complete release to the void.

Then Dimas thought of his mother and the reason he had even boarded ship in the first place—his promise to her as she lay dying—and chose to stretch his reserves as far as they might go. If death finally took him, it wouldn't be because he had surrendered to it.

Clinging to the trunk, he rolled with the storm, his body knotted with pain. He held his breath beneath the waves and filled his lungs when the surface reappeared, working with what strength he had left to outlast a force that had no measure. He had no bearings on his position, held no concept of where the shattered steamer might be, except possibly lodged against the rocks at the base of the high cliff that had appeared in the lightning.

Finally, the walls of surging waves grew smaller. The rise and fall lessened and he discovered at last that the storm had passed, had carried itself farther down the coastline and out to sea. Pieces of the steamer and clothing floated past. He waited for bodies, but saw none and didn't question it. He believed it to be a good omen on this night of terrible signs and messages.

The waters calmed more and more and he could see the moon floating edgewise in the sky. Not far ahead, the cliffs reflected the light, a soft white against their rocky outcrops. He began to kick with his feet, slowly, then stopped when he realized that the tide was taking him in anyway. Best to save what little strength he had left to get himself onto the shore, and he knew that he would make it.

The fire continued to bring Dimas warmth. It was all that kept him conscious. He had managed to catch and cook a few of the small crabs that he discovered hiding under the driftwood, having washed ashore with the storm. Still, his stomach churned with hunger. Pinch all they want, he wasn't turning them loose.

After drinking deeply from a spring that flowed from the hillside and down into the surf, Dimas had discovered a driftwood pile, where the lower layers had escaped the rain. He had used his knife to scrape kindling and his flint to strike flame in the waning moonlight. The effort had cost him precious strength, but had he failed, the cold would have taken him. His trousers had almost dried completely, but his buckskin shirt would take more time. He continued to wear it, allowing it to dry on his back, in order to keep the leather from shrinking.

His high-top leather moccasins would also need more time to dry. Made from buffalo hide—the top section of an Indian teepee, at the opening, where the covering is tempered by campfire smoke—they had served him as well as his shirt. He had learned from his father, an early trader among the Rocky Mountain Indians, that you remained cool in the summer and warm in the winter in buckskins. Also, with moccasins, you walked very quietly.

He also wanted to be certain the mechanisms of his pistol were cleaned free of mud and light debris. The desire to get it done was strong, but he was still too weak. He needed something more than the scuttling little crabs that seemed more effort than they were worth.

Dimas finished a crab and looked out over the seascape as the sun came over his back, the light flooding across water now rolling onto shore as if nothing had ever happened. Farther along the beach he could hear voices, sometimes shouting, but he had no desire to investigate. It would mean he would have to walk around a cliff above the water to see anything and despite his frustration, he needed to cook more crabs before going anywhere.

As he cleaned the shell of yet another crab, he finally regained his senses, returning to the present time and place, back from the strange watery hell of the night before. He knew it to be November in the year 1852 and that he was close enough to San Pedro to have lost little time in beginning the mission that had brought him here. That was foremost on his mind and would be until he had accomplished the task, something he hadn't asked for but had been forced to accept, nonetheless.

The change in his life had come without warning. After serving in the war, he had become a Texas Ranger for a time, until word had reached him of his mother's sudden illness at their family home in Kansas City. After meeting with her, watching her die, and attending to the funeral arrangements, all his plans had changed.

He had made a promise to her that would likely be the most important mission of his life, and he didn't know if he was up to it.

As he rested, fog rolled in off the ocean. He rose from the fire and drank again from the spring. Hearing and sensing movement, he turned toward the upland. In a moment, a small burro emerged from the haze, dragging a rope attached to its halter.

Stuffed canvas bags hung over both sides. Dimas considered that they possibly contained a fortune someone had panned from one of the creeks. Or better yet, there were provisions and food supplies.

The burro slowed to a stop, head down, sides heaving. Dimas struggled to approach it.

"Easy, little fellow," Dimas said. "Just hold on."

Dimas was aware that he was shaking. His reserves completely drained, he needed more sustenance.

He managed to secure the rope. He rubbed the burro's neck and scratched its ears, calming it. From nearby, within the fog, he heard a voice.

"Hey, there, *amigo*. You look mighty feeble."

An older Mexican man, small in stature, wearing a sombrero twice his size, used a handmade cane to approach Dimas.

"You'd make a poor *bandido*."

Dimas handed him the rope. "I couldn't find any gold in the bags." When the old man frowned, he added, "Guess your luck's the same as mine."

"People around here don't joke about gold." Then he laughed. "But it would be a good joke if I ever found any gold."

"How'd your burro get away from you?"

"Ran off last night during the storm. Been running ever since." He studied Dimas. "You were on the *Rosa Maria?*"

Dimas nodded. "Were there other survivors?"

The old man pointed beyond the cliff. "Some, I guess. A lot of dead ones washed ashore, though, and people fighting like scavengers for the belongings!

Tearing off rings and clothes and whatever has value." He reached toward Dimas and flicked a scrap of crabmeat from his lower lip. "There. You look better."

"I don't have a mirror," Dimas responded.

"Oh, yes, a mirror. That would help." He motioned Dimas toward the fire. "Come and sit down with me, and we'll get to know one another."

TWO

Dimas followed the older man to the fire. He tied his burro securely to a large chunk of driftwood and whispered something into the animal's ear.

"I told him that he's better to stay with me," he explained to Dimas, "because there are wolves about."

Dimas smiled. "He doesn't believe you."

"He'd better, because it's true. Four-legged and two-legged, both."

Percival reached into a bag and pulled out a coffee tin and two small bags. He measured rough-cut coffee beans, and water from a canteen, into the tin.

He motioned for Dimas to sit down. "Make yourself comfortable, *amigo*."

The old man set the coffee and water to brewing along one side of the fire. When coals had formed to his liking, he pulled a small frying pan from a greasy sack and filled it with frijoles and dried beef, with a little water in the bottom.

"Wish we had some fresh tortillas," he said.

"This will do fine," Dimas said. "I appreciate it."

"Ah! The least I can do for you, since you caught my wild burro for me. My name is Percival." He extended his hand.

Dimas studied him. "Percival, like the knight?"

"Don't we all have a quest of some sort?" He smiled and poured coffee.

"My name is John Dimas."

"Oh, Dimas, you say?" The old man grunted. "I thought you were in Paradise, with the Christ."

"He must have kicked me out," Dimas responded.

"Ah! You're having a hard life. Maybe you'll do good here and get back to that place, eh?"

"Not likely," Dimas responded.

"So, you are a religious man, I can see," Percival said. "You knew Dimas to be one of the two thieves crucified with Jesús."

"My mother told me, yes. The other one was Gestas—wasn't that his name?"

"That's the commonest name given him," Percival agreed. "Gestas said, 'If you are God, get us out of this mess,' and then Dimas said, 'Take me where you're going.' "

"Does it really make a difference, who was who?" Dimas asked.

"You tell me," the old man replied.

"Maybe they got it wrong. It must have been Dimas who taunted him."

Percival laughed. "I might agree. Who knows?"

They ate in silence for a short time. Dimas knew enough not to bolt his food, lest it bolt itself back out of his stomach. While he ate, he peered across the water.

"So, you wanted to die out there with the others?" Percival asked him.

"It feels odd."

"Let me tell you something. Your time's not come yet."

"I just said it feels strange, is all."

"You'll have to get over it and move on." He chewed his food loudly. "You've been through this kind of thing before, this living while others die all around you? Haven't you?"

Dimas nodded.

"We all have. At one time or another, or we've not lived."

Dimas got up and walked to the trunk that had saved him, resting on its side in the sand. Percival followed him over and, with a small pistol, shot the lock free.

"It belongs to you now," he said.

Packed inside were layers of dresses and undergarments and a smaller stack of clothes for a little girl, including pictures and hairpins and hats.

Dimas took a deep breath.

"I knew this little girl," he said. "She offered me one of her biscuits one morning."

"The Lord wanted them back," Percival said. "We already went over that." He pointed to one corner. "See, they left you a bag of gold coins to get yourself started again."

"I can't take it."

"If you don't, who will? It's meant for you."

Dimas took the bag from the trunk. He also discovered a copy of *Gulliver's Travels,* somewhat damp and dog-eared but definitely readable.

"I know this book, from my school days," he said. "I find it now?"

"You don't agree with your fate, do you?"

Dimas tossed the book down and made his way along the beach, to where a bag lay caught up in large planks and rope. He pulled the bag back to the fire. It took a while to untie the secure knot. The inside revealed two pistols and a rifle along with pouches of shot.

"Looks like your lucky day," Percival said.

"Interesting," Dimas observed, "but I don't need them."

"Put them against the cliff over there," Percival suggested.

"Do I need everything I find here?"

"Who knows what you need, or when. But don't throw all your luck away."

Dimas placed the bag against the cliff's edge and covered it with rock. "Maybe I'll be back," he said. "Who knows."

He joined Percival next to the fire. He sat back and stared across the water, then began flipping the pages of *Gulliver's Travels.*

Percival raised the coffee. "You want more?"

Dimas shook his head. "I'm good, thanks."

Percival grunted. "Let's just say that you're better."

Dimas looked at him and asked, "I still can't see why you travel this country alone."

"You've gotten nosey with your full belly."

"I'd hate to see you robbed, or worse."

Percival laughed. "Everyone worries about the wrong people."

Percival explained that as the country continued to fill with gold seekers, there would be those who got lucky, and those who would be there to take it away from them.

"Not everyone who steals is called a *bandido,*" he said. "In times like these, the powerful find ways to gain more power."

"I've come neither for gold nor power," Dimas explained.

"You have arrived at the beginning of something that will mark this land," Percival explained. "There's a vigilante committee that sits in session even as I speak to you. A man in power pushed the limits of discretion and forfeited his life for it. They will mark a man for it and it will turn this state upside down."

"I came for a purpose," Dimas told him. "I don't need to be involved in any of what you just told me."

Percival rose from his seat and walked over to the spring. He washed the cups and plates, being careful to get every little speck of food. Then he packed them into the greasy bag with the frying pan. "I hate to eat and run. I have someplace to be."

"I understand. How can I get to Los Angeles from here?"

Percival studied him. "You didn't listen to a word I said."

"I heard it all," Dimas told him. "I don't have a choice."

"We all have a choice." He pointed. "Follow the trail I came down and go north along the bluffs. San Pedro is less than a half-day's journey. There will be stages running from the port, all the time."

"Thanks for the information and the hospitality," Dimas said. "What can I do to repay you?"

"Find me some gold," Percival replied. "Or if you find me like I did you, have some fresh tortillas to go with the beans and steak."

With just over twenty passengers aboard, the small but sturdy steamer *Sea Bird,* down from San Francisco, docked at San Pedro in early morning. Clouds had gathered and a light rain had begun to fall.

Maura Walsh, dressed in a fine blue cotton dress, made her way off the ship, together with her future mother-in-law, who studied the crowd at the dock with squinted eyes.

"Well, we've finally arrived," Maura said. Her matching hat held flowing ribbons that tapered down her back, against an abundance of red-brown hair. She held a darker umbrella against the glare.

The older woman fumbled to get her own umbrella open. "I cannot understand where Trenton is," she said, stiffening with anger. "He promised me he'd be here."

"It's been a while since you've seen him, hasn't it?"

"I've seen him once since his father died, a year ago," she replied. "It would be nice if he would be more attentive to me, but I do realize he's a busy man. He's done well to become employed by one of the wealthiest men in the region."

"He says that's good for all of us," Maura offered.

"I believe that to be true," Mrs. Sterns agreed. "But you already have position. It's good to know that you have a drive toward making life better for those who are less fortunate, especially the children."

"They have their own challenges, to be sure," Maura said.

She reflected a moment on her own time as an orphan in San Francisco, after having lost both parents to illness. There had been no one to step forward to claim her, and five years of living at loose ends with other children in the same situation had taught her what survival and coping meant.

When her uncle, on her father's side, had discovered her and had taken her into his lavish estate, her life had turned completely around. No more hunger or want for the amenities of outward existence. She still longed for her parents, certainly, but the deep hole had been filled to a great degree by her uncle and his generosity. His teaching her the business of importing and exporting goods had added to her confidence and had made it possible, upon his sudden death from heart problems, to create a strong foundation for her inheritance.

"This isn't the Trenton I know. I have to think that perhaps it's the weather that's keeping him," Mrs. Sterns suggested.

"Very likely," Maura agreed. "We can make our way to Los Angeles, I'm sure. I'm confident he'll find us."

"I just don't like it, is all," Mrs. Sterns continued. "With that other ship having wrecked, you'd think he would want to be here even more."

Maura smiled. "We're here, Agnes. No need to be concerned about things that never happened."

Maura had reason to count her blessings. She had initially planned to take the *Rosa Maria* to Los Angeles but had waited an extra two days to allow her future mother-in-law to finish a business transaction in San Francisco. She had taken the time, herself, to provide for funds whenever she needed them in the Los Angeles area.

The weather along the way had remained open and the *Sea Bird* had carried them safely and smoothly down from San Francisco. Then, upon nearing San Pedro, the appearance of numerous official vessels, and a sea still dotted with floating debris, had put them on alert. News had reached the steamer of the earlier shipwreck and, until their arrival at port, everyone had wrestled with uncertainty.

Now the rain increased as the women awaited their luggage.

"I suggest we take a stage into the city and settle in at the hotel, where it's comfortable," Maura said.

"No, I think we should wait until Trenton arrives."

"How long do you feel like waiting?" Maura asked.

"Well, for heaven's sake, I don't know."

"Don't get angry with me, Agnes. He made the promise he'd be here to you, not me."

"You should be upset as well, Maura," the older woman said. "After all, you are marrying him."

"That doesn't make my life conditioned to his every move," Maura pointed out.

As she spoke, Trenton Sterns and four riders approached. Sterns, tall and slender and well dressed, jumped from the saddle and removed his top hat.

"Mother, how good to see you," he said, wrapping an arm around her. "Maura, I hope the trip was better than the present weather."

"Much," she replied, leaning into his quick hug.

Sterns explained that Don Luis Markham would have also arrived but that his coach had sustained a broken wheel partway along the journey.

"He bids his apologies," Sterns told them. "After the accident, I came as quickly as I could."

"What is our means of getting to Los Angeles?" Maura asked.

"We'll take a stage," Sterns told her. He dismissed the men who had arrived with him, telling them to inform their boss that his mother and fiancée had arrived safely and they would be en route shortly. "I know the stage isn't preferable to a coach," Sterns added, "but we'll have to make do for now."

Dimas arrived at the docks in time to see the last of the passengers disembark in an ever-increasing rainstorm. True to what Percival had told him, various means of travel awaited those interested in making their way on to Los Angeles, which included the majority of travelers who reached port.

The talk was still about the wreck of the *Rosa Maria* and the loss of life. Officials had gathered to assist those searching out loved ones. Dimas made his way through the crowd to a pair of stagecoaches, patterned after the old army ambulance design, that were destined for Los Angeles.

As he waited near one of them, he noticed a slim man in a tailored suit and two ladies, one a striking woman near his age dressed in fine blue cotton, and an older woman who Dimas decided could possibly be her mother.

A coarse group of travelers, mixed seamen and gold seekers, arrived to board the first stage. Their faces dirty and unshaven, they laughed among themselves and traded bottles back and forth. The rain had drenched their woolen garments, mixing the smell of alcohol with layers of grease and sweat.

Following the two ladies and the slim man, Dimas boarded the second stage. The older woman seated herself next to him, sliding against the opposite door as close as she could scoot.

While the first stage rang with raucous laughter, Dimas and the other three passengers sat silent. The slim man eyed him openly, while the older woman and the woman dressed in blue remained discreet.

Outside the rain began to fall even harder, and a number of Indian and Mexican vaqueros struggled to place a team of lanky and unruly mules in harness. They took position beside the mules, two in front, with lassos over the leaders, to pull them forward, and two at the side, their *riatas* raised. The mules proved tough-skinned and mean, and bolted from one side to the other, shaking the stage violently. They brayed loudly, almost a squeal, their ears flat back against their heads, their yellow teeth snapping at arms and legs and hands—anything they might nip into and draw blood.

As they brayed and squealed and kicked, the woman in blue finally ended up in Dimas's lap. The slim man immediately took her hand and arm to help her back to her seat.

"Are you all right, Maura?" he asked.

"Perfectly fine, thank you."

"Not like some stages I've been on," Dimas remarked. "A good ride even before we depart."

The slim man remarked, "Maybe you should consider riding one of those vicious mules, if you delight so in bouncing about like a ragamuffin."

"Ragamuffin is sometimes good," Dimas told him. "It keeps me alert in this country, where alertness is required."

Dimas pulled out his copy of *Gulliver's Travels* and set to reading. He kept his eyes on the page, though the angry mules still jostled the stage.

Agnes Sterns studied her son's grim expression and eyed Dimas from the side, with intense curiosity. Maura used quick glances, keeping her head averted. She tried to understand her fiancé's sudden contempt and decided that, accident or not, he didn't relish seeing her in another man's lap.

The man was dressed in a buckskin shirt and worn cotton trousers, with a large Colt revolver in a red sash around his waist. In her fiancé's mind this gave him the same qualities as the ruffians in the other coach—minus the volume of literature, of course.

Maura noted that the stranger's motion and expressions were calm and calculated, yet something about him seemed sudden and dangerous, like an explosive buried deep in a rich but mysterious mine.

Finally in full harness, the mules settled down, sides

heaving. The vaqueros sat their horses and nursed bite wounds as they discussed the merits of dead mules left for the red wolves and buzzards.

A young man suddenly appeared at Dimas's window. He lugged an apple basket filled with bottles of wine. "There's no water between here and Los Angeles," he announced. Dimas paid him two dollars apiece for four bottles. He offered one each to the other three passengers.

"Do you consider that to be proper, sir?" Trenton Sterns asked.

"You'll get thirsty before we reach Los Angeles," Dimas replied.

"Perhaps we would rather go thirsty than drink that," Sterns added. "Do you even know what's in it?"

"I would guess it's wine," Dimas replied. He selected a bottle and tasted its contents. Though not of the best vintage, it was smooth, dark red, and would definitely substitute for the lack of water.

Maura said, "Must not be too bad."

Sterns frowned. "Perhaps anything tastes good to him."

Dimas held out a bottle. "My offer still stands."

"Thank you, but no," Maura said.

Agnes Sterns spoke up. "If neither of them want any, I'll take some."

Dimas felt the bottle slip from his grasp.

Sterns leaned forward to take the wine. "Mother! What in the world are you doing?"

The older woman cradled the bottle like a newborn. "Trenton, if you desire some, ask the man for it." She turned to Dimas. "Whom should I thank?"

"My name is John Dimas. John will do fine."

"Very well, Mr. Dimas. John, if you prefer. I'm Agnes Sterns." She motioned to Maura and Sterns and introduced them.

Dimas tipped his hat. "Pleased." Now he knew the reason for the slim man's aggressive attitude, lest he be flirting with the man's future wife. "Very pleased to meet you both."

Maura nodded. Trenton Sterns scowled. Mrs. Sterns pulled the cork from her bottle and drank deeply.

"Please, Mother," Sterns pleaded.

"Listen," she said, "I don't intend to have a dry trip. Besides, I'm a bit put out with you."

"You can't blame me for things beyond my control, Mother."

"I thought you told me in your letter that Don Luis Markham would be traveling by land and much earlier. Are your plans always so disrupted?"

"Señor Markham finds the seas to be much more affording to him than the trails along the foothills of the Sierra Nevada," he told his mother. "Surely you can see that. The trails swell with *bandidos* and highwaymen. They show no mercy toward anyone they encounter."

"I didn't take your boss to be a man of fear," Agnes said, after another swallow of wine.

"That's simply not it, Mother. Don Luis has no fear of traveling inland. But stopping to fight and often to bury men takes time away from his plans. It's just far easier to travel by ship and enjoy the ocean view."

"When will we get to meet this boss of yours?" Agnes pressed.

"He's looking forward to it, Mother, rest assured. He felt badly that we arrived later than we had envisioned. Perhaps I could have come ahead."

"You might have had that in mind when you agreed to be here on time, Trenton. I speak not only for myself, but for Maura as well. After all, she is your fiancée."

Dimas had kept his eyes in his book the whole time, but had trouble stifling a snicker. Sterns looked quickly at him and turned away. Dimas had never seen anyone's face turn a darker red.

Two sailors from the ship, half drunk and getting worse, climbed atop the two stages to drive. They shouted back and forth at one another, something about whose stage was the better of the two, and whose mules were faster.

"Looks like the drivers intend to make the trip even more interesting," Dimas remarked.

The driver got down and stuck his head in the window.

"What do you say we take their money?" he asked Dimas.

"I'm in," Dimas responded.

He turned to Sterns. "You're a betting man, no?"

"No," Sterns replied. "It's not a good idea."

"What's the wager?" Dimas asked.

"Fifty dollars, gold or currency."

Dimas handed the driver a gold piece. "Why not spice up the trip?" he asked.

" 'Spice' is an unusual word for the possibilities of what could happen here," Sterns pointed out.

The driver took Dimas's wager with a smile. "Cork your bottle, *amigo. ¡Suelten los carajos!* We're letting loose for Los Angeles!"

THREE

Dimas was reminded of the chariot races in Rome, with all their glitter and festive nature, but they were not riding in chariots. These carriages were much larger, much higher, and certainly much less stable. Nevertheless, and the rain notwithstanding, they churned at breakneck speed along a muddy road that coursed its way through low hills toward Los Angeles.

One stage would pass the other, mud flying from wheels and hooves, and then the other would pass. The stages would run neck and neck for a while, before one slid on the rainy road and fell behind. Sterns held tight to Maura, who smiled, while Mrs. Sterns held her breath between drinks of wine, as more than once the stages came dangerously close to one another.

The men in the other stage roared oaths, and one threw an empty wine bottle against the side of the stage door. All the while, the drivers shouted oaths back and forth and whipped the mules to their last ounce of endurance.

They ran for a distance with the mules pulling both stages stride for stride. Dimas watched as their stage steadily gained a four-length advantage.

As they neared Los Angeles, the noise alerted every dog within at least a full mile's range. Soon packs of them ran and barked alongside.

"I'm not altogether certain we'll survive this," Mrs. Sterns suggested.

"I'll wait a while before I argue that one," Maura agreed. "We're almost to the hotel."

Dimas found himself agreeing as he held tight to the inside of the stage. He had no idea the mules could muster that kind of strength after their fight against harness. They finally began to weaken, and the driver began to shout at the team, cracking his whip repeatedly, as the second stage pulled up alongside.

The other stage suddenly slid into the side where Dimas was sitting with a resounding thud that shook both carriages. The right front wheel snapped into splinters and the stage pitched awkwardly to one side.

The mules veered off the street onto the boardwalk. The team and the stage began tearing benches and walkways and storefront displays into kindling. Maura fell into Dimas again as Sterns released her to grab hold of the stage door, his eyes wild with fear. Dimas held

Maura and struggled to grip the up-side window with his free hand as the rear wheel on the far side also broke loose. Shopkeepers, patrons, and onlookers alike scattered like barnyard chickens, and before the stage came fully to a stop, the door on the far side, as well as a portion of the coach itself, had been torn loose.

Dimas looked out to see the other stage careering down the street toward the hotel. The men inside laughed so loud it sounded like howling. Sterns's wide eyes blinked back to normal and Maura stifled a laugh.

Mrs. Sterns lay against Dimas's shoulder in a faint, still clutching her bottle tightly.

Trenton Sterns leapt from the ruins and took Maura and his mother to his side, shouting in anger about the craziness of uncivilized travel.

Dimas stepped out and noticed the driver limping off through an alley a short distance away. He had been thrown from the top and couldn't bear the shame. The mules stood with their sides heaving, their heads down in the rain. Angry storeowners gathered to glare at Dimas and threw up their hands. He did the same thing.

Sterns assisted Maura and his mother in locating their bags. When Dimas found his own bag, he discovered Sterns in his face.

"You caused this. If you hadn't accepted the offer of a wager, it wouldn't have happened."

"Did we win?" Dimas asked.

"Hardly a proper joke," Sterns replied.

As the rain lessened, they continued to gather their luggage from the mud of the street. Trenton Sterns tried to separate his mother from her wine, but his effort proved unsuccessful. She seemed more upset by that than the wreck. The sprightly older woman refused to let go of the bottle and picked clothes from the puddles with one hand. When her bag had been refilled with its soggy contents, she shoved it into her son's hands.

"Maybe if you had been on time this would not have occurred," she suggested.

They walked in silence to the Bella Union Hotel. In the lobby a porter greeted them and called others over to assist in cleaning up the bags.

"I have reserved the best rooms in the house for the two ladies," Sterns announced. He turned to Dimas. "I assume you'll be staying elsewhere?"

"The best place in town is the best place for me," he told Sterns. He tipped his hat to the two women and made arrangements at the desk for his own room. He soon discovered that the best place in town warranted no awards of merit.

The Bella Union occupied the center of town, a flat-roofed adobe structure, one story high, with a large corral in the rear that ran from the building to Los Angeles Street. Nearby, a small two-story structure housed the local paper, the *Los Angeles Star*. Aside from a unique Spanish portal in the front, there was little about the hotel to stoke any enthusiasm.

The Bella Union proclaimed itself "the Best Hotel South of San Francisco," a title Dimas took further exception to immediately upon reaching his room—a six by nine dormitory with a dirt floor and only a six-foot-high ceiling. Leaks in the roof had allowed a good-sized puddle to form in one corner. Luckily, it was away from the cot, and though he had lost nearly one-third of his living quarters, he considered himself fortunate.

Maura and Mrs. Sterns had taken rooms on the other side of the hotel. Dimas had no reason to believe he'd ever be seeing them again. However, a porter approached him with an urgent tone to his voice.

"The señora wishes to see you, Señor Dimas. As soon as conveniently possible."

"The señora, or the señorita?"

"The señora, *por favor.*"

"Is there a problem?" Dimas asked in English.

He smiled and replied in English, "Perhaps a slight matter of honor, but not too much honor."

Dimas thanked him and handed him three pesos. Mrs. Sterns and Maura were waiting outside their rooms, studying a Joshua tree from which rainwater dripped.

"What can I do for you?" Dimas asked her.

She grabbed his hand and slapped a five-dollar gold piece into his palm.

"I don't accept gratuities," she said.

Dimas stared at her. "You mean the wine? I wouldn't worry about that." He tried in vain to get her to take her gold piece back. She would have none of it.

"It was something she needed to do," Maura added. "I hope you're not offended."

"No, I'm not," Dimas told her. "Where is your fiancé?"

Mrs. Sterns answered. "He went to greet his boss, Don Luis Markham, and here they are now."

A contingent of men approached. Two Indian men, dressed in worn cotton, carried bags and were told to stop by a large Mexican. Trenton Sterns walked toward Dimas and the women with his head held high, along-side Don Luis Markham, large in stature and an established Californio.

Recipients of earlier Spanish land grants, many of the Californios had established vast haciendas and had never seen better times. No doubt Markham had profited greatly from the sudden influx of people. The demand for horses had increased considerably. Even more lucrative, the booming market for beef and leather couldn't be satisfied.

Los Angeles was a city growing faster than anyone could imagine, wealthy beyond that same imagination—not so much from the gold being mined to the north, but the demand for beef that grew without any end in sight. As of 1850, the cattle herds north of San Luis Obispo, near the midpoint in distance to San Franciso, had been depleted to the point that buyers arrived in Los Angeles daily. Merchants and *rancheros* alike reaped immeasurable profits.

Markham wore a large felt hat covered with gold and silver braiding, and a vest to match. His pants, *calzoneras,* also of Mexican design, were split down the sides, adorned with silver buttons. The large-roweled silver spurs that adorned his boots jingled loudly as he walked. The deep red sash around his waist held matching Mexican pistols, each with an eagle's head carved into the grip.

Dimas watched Markham light a cigarillo and smile at Maura.

Trenton Sterns said to Dimas, "I don't understand what you're doing here, sir, unless it is to cause trouble."

Markham blew smoke and added, "Sir, is it true?"

"On the contrary," Dimas replied.

Sterns introduced his mother and Maura to Markham. Markham puffed on his cigarillo and smiled.

"I understand that you wagered a bet to race the stages," he said to Dimas. "That placed the two women in jeopardy."

"I accepted a bet," Dimas corrected him. "No one is the worse for wear."

"It's a man's duty in this land to protect the women," Markham added. He smiled. "Wouldn't you agree?"

"It should be the same duty in any land," Dimas remarked. "But I don't see either of these women as entirely helpless. Or would you present them that way?"

Sterns glared at Dimas. "You would be well advised to mind your manners."

Markham placed a hand on Sterns's arm. "Of course he's right, Trenton. Your mother and fiancée are exceptional women. But there's no need to test them, is there? Mr.—?"

"Dimas. John Dimas. Maybe they should be allowed to speak for themselves. Do you think?"

Mrs. Sterns spoke up. "I believe our dinner awaits us."

"Mother, we're merely trying to make a point here."

Markham stepped closer to Agnes Sterns. "This is a dangerous land, Mrs. Sterns. It's not prudent to encourage every stranger you meet, do you think?"

"I suppose not," Agnes Sterns acknowledged.

Markham stamped out his smoke and called to the large Mexican. "Bestez, see that my belongings get to the coach." When Bestez had left with the Indian men,

Markham turned to Maura and Agnes Sterns and tipped his hat. "Yes, ladies, I do believe our dinner awaits us."

As they departed, Maura leaned close to Dimas. "I'm sorry about all this."

Dimas slipped the five-dollar gold piece into her palm. "Give this back to Mrs. Sterns."

"It's not mine to give," she said.

Dimas refused to take it back. "Then keep it for good luck," he told her.

Dimas finished a commendable breakfast of beef, eggs, and frijoles, with fresh tortillas, and made his way toward what everyone in town was attending. The vigilance committee that Percival had told him about was in session across from the hotel, in a small, two-room adobe house. Standing room only, including the yard outside.

Dimas watched while dignitaries crowded around Don Luis Markham, paying him their regards and discussing the impending trial. Sterns stood off to the side with some of Markham's men, craving the opportunity for an introduction to some of the Los Angeles notables. That never happened.

Finally, Markham and some of the other committee members crowded through the mass of onlookers to the inside. Markham took his place in the center of the table where the committee seated themselves. Dimas followed and stuffed himself off in one corner of the crowd to watch the proceedings.

As he looked over the crowd, Dimas noticed a man near twenty years of age, with red-blond hair that streamed out from under a dusty sombrero. His quick eyes took in everything from where he stood near the door. His earth-toned cotton attire allowed him to blend into the wall behind him.

The proceedings began. At issue was the murder earlier in the month of a prominent citizen who owned and operated a saloon near Mission San Gabriel. As leader of the state militia, as well as a Mexican War veteran and an Indian agent, General Joshua Bean had established himself as a town leader and a respected businessman. He had moved up from San Diego, where he had held the position of the town's first mayor. His brother, Roy, who would later make his name in Texas as the "Hanging Judge," and the "Law West of the Pecos," was there. He shifted in his chair near the front of the room, glaring at the prisoners, while friends worked to keep him calm. It was only when Markham himself came over for a short visit that the man finally calmed himself.

A magistrate had been appointed to oversee the interrogation of eight different witnesses. Dimas learned later that the deceased, in addition to his penchant for drink, had garnered a whispered reputation for a desire for Indian women. After a night on the town, he supposedly dragged a protesting Chumash Indian woman into his room at the mission. When one of the detainees, a man named Cipriano Sandoval, attempted to stop him, Bean had offered a strong resistance, and his life had been claimed by a pistol shot to his chest.

What was unclear was who else besides Bean, the woman, and Sandoval had been present in the room, and if someone else had arrived who did the shooting. The vigilantes had been called in to round up suspects and almost anyone of Mexican descent within any distance of the event had been brought in. Some had avoided being caught, the rumor went, and the worst of them was still out there.

A bandit named Joaquín Murrieta was said to have been one of those present during Bean's murder, or during the shooting, in any event. His whereabouts were not known, and the particulars of what had taken place, the real facts, seemed not be at issue—just who had killed Bean.

Dimas couldn't help but glance at the young onlooker he had noticed earlier. His hat was now off and he was closer to the door.

A young Mexican woman took the stand, smoothing her torn and soiled clothes. She held her right hand up while an interrogator who spoke Spanish stood nearly over the top of her, swearing her in.

"Please state your name," he said to her in Spanish.

"Ana Benitez."

The interrogator turned to the magistrate and an appointed stenographer. "She has responded, 'Ana Benitez,'" he said in English.

"We know who she is by now," the magistrate blurted. "She's been on the stand a lot already."

"This is official business, if someone's going to hang," the interrogator reminded him.

"So be it," said the magistrate. "Tell her to speak English, because we know she can."

The interrogator began a line of questioning, taking his cue from the vigilance committee. They wanted to know about Joaquín Murrieta, this missing man, a *bandido* who had inherited a band of followers after the death of his brother-in-law.

"Tell us," the interrogator asked, "was one Joaquín Murrieta present the evening of General Bean's murder?"

Ana Benitez replied, "I do not remember." Her eyes darted quickly to the onlooker standing in the doorway.

"You do not remember? Or you will not say?"

Ana Benitez pointed to one of the detainees. "That

man, Cipriano Sandoval, told me that it was he who shot the judge."

There was an uproar. The magistrate called order while the deceased man's brother, Roy Bean, rocked in his chair. Sandoval sat still as a mouse, he head bowed.

"She has testified to that before," the interrogator told the magistrate.

"I know, I've got ears, damn it!" he blurted. "I want to get to the bottom of this. Ask her again about her relationship to Joaquín Murrieta."

The interrogator turned to Ana Benitez. "Is it true that you and Joaquín Murrieta are lovers?" When the woman refused to answer, he yelled, "Answer the question!"

Ana Benitez nodded in the affirmative. Again her eyes quickly sought the red-blond onlooker.

"You stated as much before," the interrogator continued. "Why won't you do it again? Confirm it for us? Could it be that you are trying to protect this *bandido*, this Joaquín Murrieta?"

Ana Benitez wiped tears from her eyes and face. "I tell you, Cipriano Sandoval did the shooting."

"Have her sit down," the magistrate ordered. He pointed. "Call that small man at the end of the bench over there. Get him up here again."

A small man rose from where he had been seated, beside Cipriano Sandoval. The two had been talking and the magistrate had caught them. The small man stood before the room.

"You are Reyes Feliz, are you not?" the interrogator asked. He, too, looked ever so fleetingly at the onlooker near the door.

Feliz nodded and begin speaking in Spanish, throwing his arms around. The onlooker now moved to the doorway.

"What the hell is he saying?" the magistrate asked.

"He says he wants to know how many times he must get up here and tell you the same thing?" the interpreter responded. "Over and over, the same thing."

The magistrate frowned. "Ask him if he realizes that his life is at stake here."

Dimas listened to what the translator said. It was a lengthy and distorted variation on what the magistrate had spoken in English, which concluded with a threat.

"Señor Feliz," the translator said in Spanish, "you are to be hanged at noon unless you come forth with the truth."

For the first time, Feliz spoke in English, broken but clearly intelligible. "Listen to me," he told the interrogator. "I am a man of poor means. I have no reason not to tell you what I know."

The interrogator leaned into Feliz's face. "The name of the murderer, or you will hang in his place."

"I will tell you again what I know," Feliz insisted, in Spanish. "I can do no more."

The room simmered with angry, impatient voices.

"What's he saying?" the magistrate demanded.

The interrogator held up a hand. "He's getting to it, I know he is." In Spanish, he said to Feliz, "You'd better get to it now. In English. No more of this foot-dragging."

Feliz winced. At first, Dimas thought him to be a good actor. Now Dimas believed him to be brilliant.

"Do you understand what I'm saying to you?" the interrogator asked.

"Of course," Feliz told him.

"Well, we're all waiting."

Feliz cleared his throat. He shot a quick glance over at the others. Dimas was certain he saw him wink at Cipriano Sandoval.

"I know that I heard shots fired and that I saw a man run from the building, through the back way," Feliz began. "I was very frightened. I knew something bad was happening."

The interpreter's eyes narrowed. "Who was this man that you saw running away?"

"Joaquín Murrieta."

"No!" Ana Benitez cried in English. "No, not true! Not true!"

"Remove her from the court!" the magistrate bellowed.

Dimas turned to the door. The young onlooker with the red-blond hair was gone.

Two officials stepped forward and dragged the shrieking woman from the proceedings. Outside, members of the crowd beat her until a group of Mexicans, both men and women, managed to pull her away.

One of the men next to Dimas laughed. "You consort with a murderer and you'll get the same, in the end."

When the magistrate had settled the crowd, the interrogator leaned back into Reyes Feliz's face.

"Say it again, Señor Feliz—who it was you saw that night?"

Feliz, his head bowed, responded, "He was there, nearby, attending a rope trick dance. It was Joaquín."

"Louder, please, Señor Feliz."

"It was him, Joaquín Murrieta."

The interpreter turned toward the magistrate and the crowd. "You all heard him plainly. It was Joaquín Murrieta who did this thing, who killed General Joshua Bean."

Again the crowd broke into an uproar. Everyone demanded instant justice, someone to pay immediately. So, of course, the present witness had to also be held as suspect. After all, how could this man know that Joaquín Murrieta, this *bandido* with a steadily growing reputation, had killed General Bean if he, himself, hadn't witnessed it? And that made him an accessory, which was nearly as bad.

The witnesses were incarcerated, their fates to be determined later. The committee, with Don Luis Markham included, adjourned behind closed doors. Dimas eased past Trenton Sterns and out of the building, where the sun shone brightly on men gathering to look for Joaquín Murrieta.

FOUR

Maura returned from a walk and entered her room. Her bags were missing. She hurried outside and watched while the porter hauled her belongings toward a waiting carriage. Mrs. Sterns had already left her room and stood waiting at the carriage.

"Excuse me!" Maura ran after the porter and stopped him. "Where are you going with my bags?"

"*Por favor,* Señorita," he replied. "I have been ordered to take your belongings to this carriage."

"Ordered by whom?"

"Señor Sterns. It was he."

The driver had already helped Mrs. Sterns into her seat. He extended his hand to Maura.

"No, thank you," she told him.

"Come on, dear," Mrs. Sterns said from her seat. "The sooner we get going, the better."

"What is this about?" Maura asked. "I had no idea we were going anywhere."

"I'm not feeling well, dear," she said. "It would be best if we got going now."

Maura thought a moment. The wine. She did show signs of its effects. Surprisingly, only slightly, though. A woman of any age, having drunk that quantity so quickly, should be more than just partially intoxicated.

"I'm sorry to hear that," Maura said. "Is there anything I can do?"

"Getting in the coach will do for starters." She pointed toward the hotel entrance. "See there, Trenton is coming. He won't be happy. He expected us to be gone by now."

Maura didn't wait for her fiancé to reach the carriage. She met him halfway.

"Why haven't you left yet?" he asked. He took her by the arm and began escorting her back.

"First of all, I didn't know we were leaving so soon," Maura said. "That wasn't our plan."

Sterns tried to hurry her. "Everything's changed. It's a dangerous time here, with that outlaw loose."

"What outlaw?"

"Joaquín Murrieta, a *bandido* turned killer," Sterns replied. "You and mother shouldn't waste any more time."

Maura stopped him. "What about our plans?"

"Plans?"

She frowned. "Maybe I should say *my* plans—for an orphanage. You were going to help me find a suitable location and get things started, so I could begin operations soon after our wedding."

"Well, all that will just have to wait," Sterns said.

He took her by the arm again. She pulled away.

"Trent, I'm not a child."

"Then stop acting like one."

"I beg your pardon."

"It's dangerous here. Can't you understand that?"

"I'm asking you about when the danger is passed—about the orphanage."

Sterns all but pushed her up into the carriage.

"Who can say when that will be?" he replied. "Until then, do as I tell you, and nothing different."

Maura stood on the porch of the ranch house, staring into the twilight over the ocean. The headquarters at Rancho de Los Palos Verdes was situated atop a large bluff that overlooked the Pacific. Below, the mouth of a stream emptied its fresh waters in a huge fan that spread across a wide sandy beach. Agnes had drunk more wine, from Don Luis's stock, and had fallen asleep in her room, so there was no one but Maura to view the splendor of the late evening.

She had finally found it in her to relax. The constant hum of Mrs. Sterns's voice during the carriage ride from Los Angeles had tested her sanity. They had traveled the better part of the day, reaching the hacienda in late afternoon. The trip had been uneventful, with Mrs. Sterns asking Maura at first why she had so many questions about what was expected of her. Her place was to obey—didn't she know that?

Maura had ignored her, for the most part, taking in the scenery instead. The entire valley glistened a deep green with the late fall rains. Many of the shrubs had sprouted new blossoms, and many wildflowers were also going through another blooming phase as well. Wildlife took advantage of the reprieve from summer's heat. Elk and deer filled every draw, browsing and filling themselves with the luscious new growth.

But more than the wildlife, the vast herds of cattle and horses seemed endless. Vaqueros roamed among them, roping some of them or herding them from one place to another.

Her mind wandered to the image of John Dimas. Not your typical gold seeker, that she knew for certain. He seemed a man unto himself in many ways, and certainly not one to back down from a confrontation. She had thought Trenton Sterns to be a man to hold his own with almost anyone. If not physically, then certainly mentally. But he seemed taken aback by John Dimas.

Maura still found herself completely baffled by Sterns's complete change of demeanor. Except for his outward appearance, she could no longer believe he was the same man she had met and fallen in love with less than a year before.

His business trip to San Francisco, accompanying Don Luis Markham, and to see his mother at the same time, had brought them together at a formal party to honor John Bigler, the governor of California. Maura was well known in town. Her uncle, Joseph Walsh, before his sudden death, had owned a thriving import business. Having no siblings, and her mother dead five years, Maura had inherited everything.

With little to no experience in shipping and importing, Maura had sold the company for a tidy profit. She was set for life, able to begin any sort of enterprise she wished.

She had been attracted to Sterns because he had made a commanding impression on her during their first meeting, at a fund-raiser for a San Francisco orphanage, following the reception for the governor. After she had spoken in behalf of the home, detailing her own experiences of finding a deceased friend's two small daughters starving to death on the streets, he had sought her out, presenting her with a bouquet of flowers and a dinner offer to discuss a project of his own.

He had told her he had always wanted to found an orphanage himself in Los Angeles, one not connected to the Church, but a complex built in the form of a giant horseshoe, with continuous rooms on one floor that could house many orphaned and wayward children. He had told her that she seemed to be the right person with whom he might begin the project.

When Markham had returned to Los Angeles, Sterns remained behind for three months, to court Maura and further present his plans. It had all seemed so right to her at the time. Here, finally, was a man not centered solely on his own desires, but willing to contribute some of his personal wealth for the well-being of unfortunate children. That is how things had seemed until his last visit, just before leaving again on a steamer for Los Angeles the week before she and his mother left.

During the visit, he had hurried her to prepare for the move to Los Angeles and to become settled for a time at Markham's hacienda. Sterns had spoken little about the plans for the orphanage, only when she had insisted they discuss it. He seemed much more preoccupied with getting her there than anything else. When things had gotten too strenuous, he had brought her flowers and apologies and had taken her to dinner.

For some reason she had accepted all his excuses of

limited time and pressure from Don Luis Markham to return to ranch business. She had decided she would see to it herself that the orphanage would become a reality. Now, with the threat of the *bandido* Joaquín Murrieta alarming everyone, she wondered how long it would take before those plans even got underway.

Maura had decided that she would give the situation a full week before determining her next step. Perhaps the serenity of the hacienda would help. No need to jump to conclusions just yet. Better to let things flow, step back, and see which way they turned.

Dimas found himself lost among the hordes that filled the Los Angeles night. The streets glowed with light from the many cantinas along both sides. Music and laughter mixed with cursing and shouting as throngs of gamblers and sightseers elbowed their way from one establishment to the next. Spaniards, Indians, newly settled Americans, and immigrants from a multitude of countries mixed freely, having no care about what the next moment might bring them.

As he moved among the throng, Dimas wondered how Maura Walsh fit into it all. Obviously Trenton Sterns was connected to Don Luis Markham in some way, and Markham certainly fit the profile of the wealthy *rancheros* in the area, wealthy, in many cases, beyond imagination. Was this striking woman to become the wife of a cattleman's foreman?

That hardly seemed like Maura Walsh. In the short time he had known her, she had left the impression of wealth and position. There had to be some other reason, besides being Trenton Sterns's future wife, for her coming to southern California.

Inside the Tres Caballeros, Dimas ordered a shot of whiskey and gazed upon women adorned in feathers and furs who were heaping attention upon men flexing their muscles in thousand-dollar suits and filling the air with cigarillo smoke. The men lined up at monte and faro tables covered with green baize, each overseeing his own pile of $50 gold ingots that they referred to as slugs. The gamblers shoved them forward, twenty or thirty at a time, at the turn of a card.

The room might have glowed and sparkled with those tables filled with gold, but for the smoke that hung like fog over a coastal bottom. And it was that very smoke that hid the entrance of the *bandidos* and masked their intent, until they opened fire with their revolvers, adding spent gunpowder to the billows of burned tobacco.

Yells and screams filled the room. Patrons tripped over one another, falling and floundering and being trampled by others trying to find the exits. The gamblers returned fire, anxious to save their gold ingots.

Many of them fell to the invaders, either to their Colt revolvers or their sawed-off shotgun blasts.

Others were cut and sliced by machetes the *bandidos* brought down in deadly arcs, clearing pathways to the gambling tables. They shouted in Spanish as they worked, hustling from one table to the next, scooping armfuls of slugs into empty freight and mailbags.

Dimas held his revolver over his head as he weaved his way through the crowd toward the front doors. The din reminded him of battle—the echoing gunfire, and the screams and curses and the yelling—except that the pitch was much higher, accelerated by the women. Some of them fought like caged cats. He watched one painted lady run a knife into the stomach of a *bandido* who had made the mistake of tearing at her clothes. She pulled the blade across lengthwise. The *bandido*'s eyes widened with shock and pain, his hands clutching his middle in a vain effort to keep his entrails from rolling out onto the floor.

The pandemonium spread to the street. Other establishments had been hit simultaneously, and masked horsemen in sombreros and heavy chaps spurred their horses through the scattering crowd, firing their pistols, their bags of loot jingling as they passed. Over the din came intermittent shouts: "Joaquín! It's Joaquín!"

Dimas took a stand against the wall of a general

store. A group of horsemen started past, firing their pistols at him. He moved and ducked, returning their fire, balls whining in the air, splinters of wood flying all around him. One rider doubled over in the saddle and another fell to the ground, flopping like a fish in the street. Two of his *compadres* returned for him. Dimas took cover behind a horse trough as one of them emptied two pistols at him, while the other fastened a noose under the fallen man's arms. Soon they were gone in the darkness, dragging the fallen man behind them.

Dimas came out from cover. He switched cylinders in his revolver and spun the full load to be certain the action was clear. More *bandidos* ran their horses through the streets, yelling loudly and gaining speed until they reached him.

He emptied his revolver, knocking three from their saddles. Two appeared dead, a third came to his knees. The crowd collapsed on him, knives gleaming in the flaring light that streaked the shadows. The *bandido* barely had time to yell.

The sun fell down and the stars shone above like an eternity of diamonds. Maura stepped off the porch to better view them, at the same time listening to the rushing surf below, thinking to herself that the darkness felt comforting.

She heard the clinking of spurs and jumped to one side as a hand touched her shoulder.

"Señorita, are you quite comfortable?"

"Don Luis, what a surprise."

Markham blew smoke from a cigarillo. "This is indeed a very good place to think, don't you agree?"

"It's beautiful here. And, yes, very serene."

Markham stepped toward her. "I just didn't think you should be alone. Not in all this beauty."

Maura took a step away. "I was wondering where Trenton is," she said quickly. "Do you know?"

"He will be along shortly. He's in town, seeing to business affairs."

"So late in the evening?"

"I have property in town as well. With the threat of a raid by Joaquín, he is working a little past our usual schedule."

"This Joaquín fellow sounds like a very bad man."

"The worst. And getting bolder in his tactics." He blew smoke from his cigarillo. "I'm afraid all of California will not be able to rest until he is stopped. If he's not, things will only get worse."

"I had no idea it was so dangerous here."

"Ah, but you'll be protected," Markham promised. "You are right, he should not have left you. But I told him to, so he does as I wish." He laughed. "He knows that as long as you're with me, you cannot be harmed."

"With you?"

"Here, at my headquarters. I'm sure you will find yourself very comfortable, no?" He blew more smoke into the air. "As you can see, I've done a great deal to make it the best hacienda in all of California. I had the redwood brought from the forests to the north. The rock for the fireplace as well. When the weather turns cooler, you will smell the sweet cherry wood that I use, and the peach and hickory. What is your favorite?"

"I really don't have a favorite, Don Luis."

"Surely you must. Surely there are many things that you desire." He took another step toward her. "If I were Trenton Sterns, I would treat you like a queen."

"I'm quite tired," Maura said. "I believe I'll take my bed for the evening."

"I'm certain it's been a long, hard day, and your trip by steamer couldn't have been too restful," Markham said. "I'll bid you a good night."

Maura entered the ranch house and made her way down the hallway to her room. Inside, she closed the door, still feeling unsafe. None of the doors had locks of any kind. She looked out the window to see Markham staring up toward her.

She backed out of the window and blew out the lantern. She stood for a time, listening to Markham's voice, commanding in tone. Curious, she edged to the window and peered out. Below, Markham had over a dozen women lined up in front of him, Indian women selected from the ranch help. They all stood at attention, as if soldiers at inspection, while he went back and forth along the line, speaking in Spanish. He stopped now and again to feel a breast or to reach his hand under a dress. Finally, he selected two and dismissed the others.

Maura watched while he led the two up the hill to the ranch house. She could hear him, his spurs clinking loudly, his commanding voice loud, as he led the women past her door and farther down the hall.

She did not undress for bed, but lay on top of the covers. She wondered if the loud voice and the slapping sounds and the crying from down the hall would ever end.

Dimas reloaded his revolver and also two extra cylinders, making certain that the powder and lead balls were tightly packed. He needed no misfires on a night like this. The streets remained filled with confused people, but the initial shock of the raid would soon wear off. Vigilantes were already forming, and men were being recruited from the gathering crowds.

Dimas decided his mission might be parallel to theirs in some ways, but his success would not lie in joining them. Best to return to the hotel and judge his plans from a different perspective.

He started back toward the Bella Union, making his way carefully. As he rounded the corner of a building, he noticed two men bending over an older man lying on his side, groaning. A third man straddled the old man. All three turned to stare at Dimas. With his pistol drawn, Dimas shouted and started toward them. The three fled into the night.

Dimas lowered himself to one knee and saw that the old man clutched a bloody hand over his side.

He spoke in Spanish. "Can you hear me?"

The old man opened his eyes. "I have nothing for you to take," he replied. "You going to stab me, too?" The old man laughed. "Ha! It's you!"

Dimas finally recognized Percival. "How bad is it?" he asked. He helped him to a sitting position.

"Don't worry, just get me out of here. I'll show you where my daughter lives."

Percival described a small boardinghouse a ways back from the city's center. Dimas took an arm over one shoulder. When they arrived at the door, he knocked loudly.

"Her name is Elisa," Percival said. "I hope she doesn't come with a gun."

Two small boys pushed the door open. One of them struggled to hold a rifle level.

Dimas shoved the barrel of the rifle to one side. "Where's your mother?" he asked.

A young Mexican woman appeared, also holding a rifle.

"You aren't short on weapons," Dimas said. "I have your father here. He's been knifed."

"Papa!" She rushed out the door and put her hands on the old man's face. "Is it you? What has happened?"

"Somebody thought I was a rich don," he replied, lowering himself into a rocker on the porch. "Don't I look it?"

She frowned. "I thought you were away for a while."

"I'm not away. I'm stabbed, that's what I am." He grunted.

"Come inside and lie down on your bed."

"No, not yet."

"Papa, it would be better if you rested."

"It would be better, Elisa, if you put your boys to bed."

Dimas spoke up. "I found your father not far from here. Joaquín Murrieta and his bandits attacked the gaming tables tonight."

Percival turned to Dimas. "Why do you say that it was Joaquín?"

"Because people were yelling his name."

"And does that mean it was truly him?" The old man frowned deeply.

"No one could tell for sure, I guess," Dimas agreed. "They all wore masks."

"That's the point. Joaquín and his men don't wear masks. They never have."

Dimas stared at him. "How do you know this?"

"Take my word for it."

It was Dimas's turn to frown. "Have you been someplace where Joaquín raided? Have you seen him? Do you know him?"

Percival grunted. "You ask far too many questions. What I told you is true: Joaquín and his men do not wear masks. They blacken their faces. Leave it at that."

Elisa studied Dimas. "And who is this man, Papa?" she asked. "Maybe he's one of them."

"This is John Dimas, who was aboard the *Rosa Maria*."

She clasped a hand to her mouth and touched the crucifix of the large wooden rosary around her neck. "God have mercy. The shipwreck."

"Yes, the shipwreck." He struggled with the pain of a deep breath. "You remember me talking about him?"

"I thought you were making it up, like you often do."

"Not this time. Here he is. Now, I've had enough of the night air."

Dimas and Elisa worked together. The two boys, when told to by the old man, adjourned to a nearby room. The youngest, whose name was Manuel, stared at Dimas and said, "I'm glad you found my grandfather. We thought he was gone and was never coming back."

"Go on with you!" Percival told him, then insisted on being helped to a kitchen chair, still not his bed.

"You need to be in bed," his daughter insisted.

"Get me into the chair, Elisa," he told her. "You're always so pushy about things."

Dimas helped her and said, "I'll be gone and leave your father to your care."

"You haven't been excused yet," Percival said. "Sit down at the table with me. Elisa, fix us something to eat."

"Papa, you need rest, not food."

"I need food, then I'll rest. Now get to it."

FIVE

Dimas ate and listened while Percival talked of the early days and how everything had changed. Now everyone knew of this place of perpetual sun, a paradise of warm days followed by soft nights blessed with southern winds off the sea, but a place now blighted by a form of obsession known to control even the strongest of men.

"Gold drives them," he said. "It's the only meaning to life in the foothill country. The Sierra Nevada swarms with newcomers."

"Not everyone can get rich," Dimas commented.

"For a time, I was one of them," Percival admitted. "I lost track of the hours I spent with a pan in the streams. Even when the others played cards or drank or attended fandangos, I stayed in the streams and washed gravel by lantern light. It might rain or even snow at times, or the wind might blow, but I would always be wading in the streams.

"If I was lucky, I might see a few ounces per week. More often, that amount was measured over a month's time. I never saw enough to get more than a change of clothes and a stash of frijoles, maybe some bacon, and a bottle, or perhaps a good horse once in a while, for riding to other diggings that had just opened up, promising something more. There was always something more. I always had hope."

"What made you give it up?" Dimas asked.

"A miner's tax, imposed on everyone but the Yankees who came here and shoved us off our claims," he replied. "How could I pay twenty dollars a month? You know about that tax, don't you?"

"I'm new here, and not after gold," Dimas told him.

Percival laughed. "If not after gold, then what?"

"I came to find Joaquín Murrieta."

Stunned, Percival asked, "Why? To end your life?"

"I promised my mother that I would find him, as she lay dying."

"You're related to Joaquín?"

"No, but I have reason to believe that my younger brother rides with him."

Percival and Elisa stared at Dimas. "Ah!" Percival blurted.

The two boys suddenly appeared from the adjoining room, their eyes wide. Manuel blurted in Spanish, "Your brother rides with Joaquín? Are you going to ride with him, too?"

Percival growled, "You two, who told you to come back out?"

The boys smiled at Dimas and disappeared.

"You have two friends for life," Percival told him.

"I can see that Joaquín is loved," Dimas said, "but it's a good way for my brother to get killed."

"Are you sure he hasn't been already?"

"No, I'm not sure. You see, I said the rosary with my mother, bead for bead, as she passed on. I promised her that I would search for Ricardo until I found him. That I would take him out of danger."

Percival made the sign of the cross over his chest. "May your mother rest in peace. And why do you think your brother's with Joaquín?"

"He wrote my mother a letter, from San Francisco, a year ago, and another from Stockton just a month later. In them both he said that he would become famous in time, riding with an outlaw who would change all of California."

"That would be Joaquín Murrieta," Percival said. "He's the main leader. How much he wants to change and how much change he actually brings about may not be the same."

"I need to find him, so that I can learn of Ricardo," Dimas said.

"A man's fate is left to himself," Percival said. "No matter what you promised your mother, you may not be able to change his thinking. That is, if you ever do find him."

"I'll find him," Dimas said with certainty.

"You know," Percival said, "there are five Joaquíns. All related. Your brother could be with any one of them."

"You just said he was with Joaquín Murrieta."

Percival squinted. "I said that?"

"You said that Joaquín Murrieta was considered to be the leader and the one to create change. That's what my brother wrote to my mother."

Percival put a finger to his lips, his eyes wide. He pointed to a window, where a man's face suddenly appeared, then disappeared.

Everyone became quiet, except the boys in the other room, who laughed and giggled. The old man motioned his daughter to see to it that they hid themselves. He reached under a cloth on the table and pulled out two revolvers. He threw one to Dimas and cocked the other one.

"We'll see now if you can shoot," he said and blew out the lantern.

Dimas pulled his own pistol and cocked them both.

He listened intently. Elisa and the boys were in the bedroom and very quiet. He could hear the low whispers of men just outside the door.

Suddenly they were inside. Four of them charged into the room, firing wildly.

Dimas opened fire and three of them turned in circles and fell to the floor. The last one shot toward where Dimas had been, but he had moved, throwing himself across the room to a far wall. He fired again and again. The man ran through the open door, yelling, "I'm killed! I'm killed!"

Dimas stood up in the darkness. Spent gunpowder filtered out through the open door like a strange, dark fog.

"By all the saints in heaven!" Percival said. "I never got a shot off. Never even had to."

"There are more of them," Dimas told him.

He slipped out to look up and down the street. From the bedroom inside came Elisa's scream.

Dimas hurried back through the main room and into the bedroom. Elisa held herself as a shield in front of the boys. A man was trying to get through the window but was hung up on his gun belt. He swore at Dimas and fired.

The ball whined past Dimas's right ear. He fired with both pistols and the intruder jerked and dropped his revolver. With a gasp he slumped forward, hanging limp from the window.

Elisa was crying. Dimas did what he could to console her. "Find Papa," she said. "Please, find Papa."

Dimas hurried to the table. Percival was no longer under it.

"Is he there?" Elisa asked.

Dimas lit the lantern. The room was empty. Elisa held the two boys close to her and sobbed. The boys stared at him with big brown eyes.

"Elisa, where did your father go?" Dimas asked.

"He left, because he knows they will come looking for him." Her eyes took on a hard glare. "Do you know of Don Luis Markham?"

"I know who he is, yes."

"It was his men who raided the gaming tables tonight. Not Joaquín Murrieta."

"How do you know this?"

"Because my father has been watching Markham and what he does for some time. He knows too much."

"So, he's been on the run from Markham."

"Markham is corrupt and dangerous in every way," Elisa told him. "He robs and kills and is content to have everyone blame the raids on Joaquín. Though Joaquín raids and steals also, he is different. He's been accused of killing and raping women, but he doesn't do that.

Not even Yankee women. My father tried to tell the authorities, but they wouldn't listen. They even put him in jail for a time."

"Why didn't he tell me that he rode with Joaquín?" Dimas questioned.

"Is he supposed to trust everyone? Who isn't looking for Joaquín?" She clutched her two sons closer to her side. "Markham has tried every means to catch my father. But he doesn't know my father at all. No one really does."

"I don't understand."

"You will in time. He chose you, Señor Dimas, to have as a friend. He must see something special in you."

"When will he be back?" Dimas asked.

"Who can say? Don't look for him. When the time is right, you two will meet again."

"I still don't understand."

"He found you after the shipwreck, didn't he?" Elisa responded. "That is how he does things."

Suddenly the dead man in the window began to move. Someone was pulling him out from the alley.

Elisa screamed. Swearing voices rose from the other side of the wall. Dimas grabbed the dead man's collar and shirt and held tight.

"Take the boys out of the room," he told Elisa. "Hurry!"

Dimas held on until Elisa and the boys had left. He

released his grip and the body slipped out through the window. Men from the other side opened fire. Lead balls tore holes in the opposite wall. Dimas waited until one of them stuck his head in, and shot him in the face.

Dimas rolled away toward a corner as another hail of fire poured through the window. Just as suddenly the shooting stopped.

Dimas heard the pounding of horses racing away in the darkness. The two boys rushed into the room.

"Señor Dimas!" the oldest one yelled. "Are you shot?" They both hurried to him.

"I'm not shot," Dimas said. He lit a lantern and sat down on the bed.

Elisa stood back, tears streaming down her face, while the boys hugged Dimas and thanked him for saving them.

The older boy, Francis, spoke for the first time. "Joaquín will be glad to have you," he said.

Dimas returned to where Percival had been sitting. "I don't understand," he said. "I don't see any blood from his wounds."

"Perhaps he didn't bleed too much," Elisa ventured.

"He bled a lot, from what I could see." He dismissed the issue and turned to her. "You know you can't stay here. You can use my room at the hotel. I'll get another one."

"You are being too good to us." She looked hard at

Dimas. "You had better pray that none of these men that came saw you very well, or Markham will send his men after you, also."

Don Luis Markham paced in front of the main house. Sterns and Bestez and the others should have arrived from the raid well before now. They should already be unloading the gold taken from the gambling tables.

He stomped on his cigarillo and, as a contingent of horsemen approached, retrieved another from his pocket and lit it.

Trenton Sterns led the riders into the ranch yard. He reined in his horse and dismounted.

"It was a very good take, Don Luis," he said. "Very good."

Markham walked among the horses and mules, feeling the laden bags. He returned to Sterns.

"Is everything you took here?"

"Everything, yes. You know I wouldn't hold out on you."

"I know you wouldn't. Of course. Where's Bestez?"

"Close behind," Sterns replied.

Markham ordered the men to unload the mules and motioned Sterns aside. "You and I must talk."

"What's the problem? Is my mother acting up?"

"Give her some wine and she sleeps like a baby," Markham replied.

The two walked together to the bluff overlooking the ocean. Below, the surf rushed across the beach while overhead a crescent moon broke the darkness. Clouds billowed across the skies, racing in uneven patterns.

"What took you so long?" Markham demanded.

"You told me to be certain Bestez and the men got rid of the old man. Remember?"

"Is it done?"

"It took longer than we anticipated."

"I said, did you get it done?"

"No. Three of the men found him and had him down when a stranger came along and broke it up."

Markham began to pace. "What stranger?"

"I don't know who it was. Bestez and five others went to the daughter's boardinghouse to finish the job. The stranger must have been there. All were killed but Bestez, who said that a *pistolero* shot everyone."

"Did Bestez see this *pistolero?*"

"No. He was waiting with the horses. Percival got away."

Markham cursed. "That old man has too much on me. I can't afford to have him alive."

"He will not remain alive," Sterns promised.

"There is no question that he will not remain alive!"

Markham continued to pace. "Who is this stranger, this *pistolero?*"

"One of the men said that he was in attendance at the hearings," Sterns replied.

Markham laughed. "Yes, he and the rest of the town."

"Percival must have known him somehow," Sterns suggested. "Maybe hired him?"

"That old man is penniless," Markham remarked. "It makes no sense." He chewed on his cigarillo and spat. "I'll talk to Bestez when he gets here. For now, you go back to your woman. You leave her alone too much."

SIX

Sterns knocked on Maura's door and let himself in. She had fallen asleep, in her dress, on top of the covers.

She jerked awake. "Who is it?"

"Maura, why aren't you in bed?" He lit a lantern.

"I didn't feel like undressing," she replied.

"What?"

"I don't intend to be here alone again, ever."

"Maura, there was a raid on the gambling houses tonight," Sterns said. "I was needed to protect Don Luis Markham's interests in town. Joaquín Murrieta robbed and killed and caused general mayhem."

"That's terrible," Maura said. "I guess it's good that you had your mother and me come out here right away."

"It was a very good thing that I insisted, yes," Sterns concurred. He grew smug. "You should learn to listen to what I tell you."

"Perhaps so, Trent, but, nonetheless, I won't be left alone around Don Luis again. I mean that."

Sterns sat down on the bed. "What's the matter? What happened?"

"How well do you know him?"

"I know him quite well. He's very honorable."

"You're certain of that?" She watched Sterns frown and added, "I have a suggestion. Ask him if he would sleep with me, if given the chance."

"Maura, what is this about?"

"I'm saying that you're a fool to trust that man. I don't know if you can't see it, or if you don't care. Either way, it's not good."

"He has to be tough to operate the kind of business he does."

"Tough is one thing, brutal and inconsiderate is another," Maura insisted. "How did you even get mixed up with him?"

"You know that I once worked as an assistant to the governor. Don Luis has always been a staunch supporter."

Maura stood up. "Trent, I want you to listen to me for a change. If you're dismissing what I just told you, then we have serious problems."

"Maura, you've been under a lot of stress."

"Nonsense. I came here because you promised me that you would seek out a place for me to start an orphanage. You said it was your dream as well. Now you say we have to wait for that to happen."

"So, you want to die at the hands of this *bandido*, Joaquín Murrieta? Or worse, be captured by him?"

"Why have you never mentioned this man before, Trent?" she asked. "If he is such a problem, why didn't you warn me about him early on?"

"No one knew that he was in the area. Up until now he's just been a petty thief. But since his murder of General Bean, and the raid tonight in town, he's considered very dangerous."

Maura turned and stared out the window, to where the moon hung over the ocean. None of it made sense.

"Can't you see the danger everyone is in?" Sterns continued.

"When I first met you, and got to know you, things were different," Maura said. "You showed me a lot more consideration. I don't know what this is all about and how to take it all."

Sterns eased himself over to her, placing the palm of his hand on her lower back.

"Maura, I beg for your patience. We'll have our own place before long, but for a short while I have additional business to attend to. It will mean a better life for us. I hope you can see that."

"It's not that I don't realize that you want the best for us, Trent," she said. "It's that you didn't discuss it with me. There's no way for me to understand what all of this is."

"Maybe I should provide you with a daily list of what I have to do."

"Just take the time to say a few things, Trent. Is that too much to ask?"

"You're going to have to learn that I can't take the time to explain everything to you."

Maura stepped away from him. "And why is that?" she asked. "Why have you decided not to include me?"

"I told you, because I can't take the *time* to do it, Maura. That's why."

"Maybe you never had any real interest in what we discussed before." She studied his face. "Maybe it was all a ruse to get me here."

"Maura, that's not fair."

"Why did you bring me here, Trent? Los Angeles is nothing like San Francisco."

"So, you don't like the city?"

"Trent, what kind of resources are available to make large-scale development plans?" she asked.

"The city is growing. In time, Maura."

"Why did you tell me that anything I wanted was possible right away? I could have made different plans. We could have gotten married up there."

"You'll get used to it here, Maura," Sterns told her. "It will grow on you."

"And you expect me to get used to Don Luis as well?" she demanded. "Would it be good for us, Trent, if I allowed him into my bed?"

Sterns hesitated. Maura stepped farther back.

"Let's get married. It will change then," he replied. "We'll take a long honeymoon and then get busy on the orphanage. What do you say?"

"Why put the orphanage off? I have a feeling that if I don't get you to keep your word to me right away, you will never keep it."

"This is nonsense, Maura."

"Nonsense or not, I will not marry you until the orphanage is operating." Sterns stepped toward her and Maura held out her hand to stop him. "I'm serious, Trent. The date can easily be changed. I have no one who will attend. They are all your friends."

Sterns took a deep breath. He realized he had lost the battle completely and was on the verge of losing the war.

"Okay, listen," he said. "There's a boardinghouse in town that is going to be used as a temporary quarters for some kids coming down from the mines. Why don't we see if you can get involved in that? What do you say?"

"A boardinghouse?"

"It's run by a Mexican woman named Elisa, who has two young boys. The Church asked her if she would do it for the time being. She's amenable to it. I'm sure she'd welcome the help you could offer."

"How did you learn of it?"

"Don Luis gives to the Church, of course. He does more than tithe."

"It's good to have the Church fooled," Maura commented. "Why shouldn't he be a pillar of the community?"

"Aside from your opinion of Don Luis Markham," Sterns said, "what do you think of my idea regarding the boardinghouse?"

She thought a moment. "We could look into it."

"Good, now let's get to bed." He came toward her again.

"Trent, you seem to be pushing aside the fact that Markham made advances toward me. It doesn't bother you at all?"

"I'm not sure that he did, Maura. Maybe you just misunderstood him."

Maura took a deep breath. "We're going in to check into that boardinghouse, first thing tomorrow."

"I'm not sure it can be that soon, Maura."

"Then let me say it this way. With or without you, I'm going into town tomorrow. I'm not certain that I'll be coming back. Maybe I'll just go on back to San Francisco."

"I'll see to it that the port at San Pedro is blocked to you," Sterns warned.

"I'm getting to know the real Trenton Sterns, I believe. I suspect my fortune could have done you a great deal of good."

Sterns worked to compose himself. He needed her kind of financial backing to make his way into the high political circles he had always desired so strongly.

"Maura, we can work this out."

"Perhaps. Perhaps not, but not tonight."

From outside came the sounds of approaching horsemen. Sterns hurried to the window.

"I have to leave for now, Maura." He pulled his shirt out and unbuttoned it.

"I see." Maura watched while he tousled his hair. "When you greet Markham, it has to look like we've done something here."

Sterns swung past her. He slammed the door and was gone.

Maura moved to the window. Markham stood in the yard awaiting the riders. She turned her eyes toward the ocean and its calming effect, except that she couldn't become calm. She had gotten herself into something she had been very blind to in the beginning.

Don Markham greeted Bestez and two other men on horseback in Spanish. They led two horses with a body draped over each saddle.

"You know the rules, Bestez," Markham said.

Bestez drew a breath. "Would you have us leave him in the window for someone to identify at first light?"

"How did that happen?"

"He was trying to climb into that boardinghouse to find Percival and some *hombre* dressed in a buckskin shirt killed him, shot him from close range."

"Sterns said he was a *pistolero*?"

"He was a deadly one, yes. I didn't see him well, though."

Trenton Sterns arrived, tucking his shirttails in. Markham waited for him to approach and said, "You didn't have to stop what you were doing and get dressed for this."

Sterns laughed. "I told her to wait up for me and we'd finish."

Markham got back to business. "We have to find this *pistolero* everyone is talking about. An *hombre* in a buckskin shirt."

Sterns straightened up. "A buckskin shirt."

"He wore buckskin, yes," Bestez acknowledged.

"I believe it's the same man we met in the hotel courtyard," Sterns told Markham. "Do you remember? When we went to meet Maura and my mother."

"Yes, at the Bella Union. John Dimas. I do remember him."

"Maybe he's at the hotel now." Sterns suggested.

"We have two men to find," Markham told him. "Percival and this John Dimas. But Dimas is foremost. Go to the Bella Union tonight and bring him to me. Understand? I want to meet this man again—this *pistolero*. I want to talk to him very badly."

"Bestez and I will lead some men in to get him, Don Luis," Sterns promised. "You will get another meeting with him."

Dimas lay awake in his bed. He sorely needed rest, but it was impossible to come by. He felt weak yet energized at the same time, staring alert at the ceiling.

Outside, the night had quieted to a degree. Dawn was breaking and at this point the gunfire was only sporadic. Dimas had checked out the entire area before taking Elisa and the boys back to the Bella Union. He had settled them as best he could in his old room, waiting until she and the boys were lying down and resting. Elisa had brought a candle with her, and when Dimas left, it was burning on a nightstand beside the bed.

Elisa had insisted he take her rosary and place it around his neck. "I know the Blessed Virgin will protect me and my boys," she told him. "Since you helped my father, it's you they want now." Manuel had shaken his hand with a broad smile, saying, "You can sleep well because you will soon be riding with Joaquín."

Dimas sat up and rubbed his face with the palms of his hands. From the distance came the sound of galloping horses.

He hurried to his old room and knocked loudly before entering. Inside, the candle was still burning.

Elisa held her boys close, and they all rose to their feet.

"What is it?" Elisa asked.

"Somebody's here and I don't have a good feeling about it," he replied. "We haven't much time."

Elisa ushered her two boys past him and they followed Dimas into the shadows, along the hotel's outer walls, and through the adjacent alleyways, while close behind Markham's men began searching rooms and disturbing guests in the area where Dimas had stayed. He could hear Sterns's loud voice, insisting that a man named John Dimas was very bad, and that this man was suspected of being a *bandido* who rode with Joaquín Murrieta.

As the light began to widen over the horizon, Dimas took Elisa and the boys back toward her boardinghouse. Behind, Sterns and Bestez were gathering the men.

Elisa clutched the boys close. "They're coming this way."

They reached the boardinghouse to discover two Franciscan priests, along with over twenty young children, all wearing ragged clothing, standing just outside the door. They all turned at once.

The older of the two priests stepped toward them. "I'm Father Francis and this is Father Manuel. We have traveled a long way. Is this your place we've come to?"

Elisa hurried to him and clutched his robe. Tears rolled down her cheeks.

"Father, praise the Blessed Virgin and all the saints, I'm so very glad you've arrived."

"What is it, child?" he asked.

Both priests took note of the rosary around Dimas's neck. They stared a moment at the pistols in his sash.

Dimas looked back up the street. Sterns and Bestez were leading Markham's men, riding at a full gallop toward the boardinghouse.

"We've had some trouble, Father," Elisa said. She pointed. "Those men want to take my two boys and sell them as slaves."

Both priests frowned.

"It's true." She made the sign of the cross. "Last

night, they came for the children and shot people inside of the house. We had to run from here."

Father Francis pointed at the approaching riders. "You are certain it was those men?"

"Very certain, Father," Elisa insisted. "I cannot forget their faces, or what they wanted to do."

"How did you get away from them?" Father Manuel asked.

Elisa motioned toward Dimas. "The Lord works in mysterious ways."

The priests herded Elisa and all the children inside and closed the door. Both priests exclaimed at the bloodstains on the floor.

Father Francis instructed the eldest children to take the smaller ones into the back rooms and remain there. Outside, Sterns and Bestez led Markham's men into the yard and reined in their horses.

"Who did you say they are?" Father Francis asked.

Elisa looked to Dimas. If she spoke the truth, the padres would have trouble believing her.

Dimas replied for her. "They work for Don Luis Markham."

"What?" Father Francis exclaimed.

"Child stealers?" Father Manuel added. "How can that be possible?"

"Don Luis must not know what they are up to," Dimas added. "He would be very angry if he knew."

"Yes, he would, at that," Father Francis concurred. "There is no possible way Don Luis Markham could tolerate such actions."

The younger padre spoke up. "We made better time than we had expected. It was the will of Christ Jesús we get here to stop this."

Father Francis made certain the children were well back into the rooms off the hallway. He looked to Dimas.

"God forbid there should be any shooting."

"God forbid," Dimas said.

Father Francis opened the door and stepped outside, the younger priest behind him. Dimas watched carefully through a window.

Father Francis and Father Manuel both studied Sterns and Bestez and the others.

"It's very early for a hard ride to a boardinghouse," Father Francis began.

Sterns stated that they were after a man dressed in buckskin—a *pistolero,* likely one of Joaquín Murrieta's men, who had robbed and killed the night before.

"He is a very dangerous man," Bestez added. "He would even kill a priest."

"I've been told something different," Father Francis said. "The young woman claims that you are after her children."

Sterns and Bestez frowned.

Father Francis put an edge to his voice. "Selling children like that is a mortal sin, and punishable by eternal damnation. Did you know that?"

Sterns said, "Someone has told it to you wrong, Father."

"Oh, well, I wonder," Father Francis countered. "The young woman's boys are very frightened, so I believe them. And you wouldn't want Don Luis to learn that you tried to steal young boys."

"I told you," Sterns argued, "we're after a *pistolero* dressed in buckskin. His name is John Dimas."

"It doesn't matter what you told me, my son," Father Francis said sternly. "What matters is what I'm going to tell you." He turned to the younger priest. "Father Manuel, you are witness to this."

Father Manuel bowed. "I am a witness, as you wish, Father Francis, in the name of Christ, Jesús, our Savior and Lord."

"I want you to hear what I tell these men, so that they will realize they cannot do the evil things they want to do."

"I'm listening, Father."

Bestez spoke up. "I don't wish to go against the Church."

"Good," Father Francis said. "Now, you men go back to herding horses and cattle, and doing for Don Luis Markham what God intends you to do. Don't make me call on Don Luis to settle this matter with you. Or perhaps that would be best?"

Sterns spoke quickly. "There is no need to involve Don Luis, Father. We'll leave here now, if that's your request."

"It is my request."

"But I must warn you of the danger you could be in," Bestez put in. "The *pistolero*."

"Perhaps we should pay a visit to Don Luis," Father Manuel suggested. "To discuss this matter."

Sterns and Bestez both sat frozen in the saddle.

"Perhaps that would be wise," Father Francis concurred.

Sterns turned his horse and the others followed. When they had left, the two priests entered the house.

Elisa wiped tears away. "You have saved us, both of you," she said.

"It is our duty," Father Manuel told her.

Father Francis approached Dimas. "Who gave you the rosary?"

"Elisa did, for protection."

"It has served you well today," the priest said. "Now take it off, please. *Pistoleros* need all the prayers anyone can spare, but such a man is not allowed to wear items of that sort."

Dimas handed the crucifix to the priest. "I do appreciate the help, Father."

"Did you kill anyone while wearing it?"

"No, Father."

"Very good." He handed the crucifix back to Elisa, and turned back to Dimas. "Would you like to have your confession heard, my son?"

"That would be good," Dimas replied. "Very good." They began a slow walk through a nearby vineyard. "Before we get started, I have a question."

"By the look on your face, it would seem to be a very troubling one."

"I made a promise and it wasn't something I had thought out well beforehand," he said. "I shouldn't have made it in the first place."

"A man is only as good as his word."

"True, but there is reason to believe the promise could cost me my life, and that there is likely no chance in fulfilling it anyway."

The priest stopped walking. "Then why would you consider such a promise in the first place?"

"I wanted to make an older woman happy in her last moments before death."

"Forfeiting your life would make this person happy?"

"No, the hope of me saving a life was her dying wish—her youngest son."

Father Francis studied him. "To make such a promise you would have to be the woman's son as well. Is that true?" When Dimas nodded, he added, "I should advise you, your confession must be as solemn and complete as any you have ever given."

SEVEN

For the remainder of the day, Dimas avoided the Franciscans. They did not intend to take him to task regarding the allegations against him by Markham's men. Instead, they made their determinations of him based on the children, who wouldn't leave him alone.

Dimas agreed to be led around by the hand and given a tour of the facilities by Elisa's two sons. Francis found it fascinating that he and the older priest shared the same name.

Though the boy realized he had been given the name of the famous saint from Assisi, who had become the patron of animals and the earth, he liked to imagine that his own worth was at least equal to that of his namesake.

Manuel delighted in exclaiming to the other children that Señor Dimas was a member of Joaquín's band and had come to help them when they had needed it. Perhaps there were occasional saviors among those who ordinarily trampled over anyone they deemed to be in their way.

Despite their collective problems, which had taken a high toll emotionally, the other children found a kind of solace in having Dimas with them. Too few adults, their parents included, had treated them with any form of dignity.

Theirs was a world of complete confusion, with nowhere to turn save the charities offered them from those willing to help. Every gold camp generated them and in Los Angeles, their numbers had grown by leaps and bounds. Parents were killed or injured and, in many cases, were too poor to feed extra mouths and took them to other families to be kept, or to the few orphanage homes that could be found.

Though Dimas had never been orphaned, he could relate to kids at loose ends, searching for stability in their lives. With his father off trapping in the mountains for extended periods of time, and his mother most often at the church wearing out her rosary, he had a lot of time to himself, and time with Ricardo, when his younger brother was open to it.

That was seldom, if ever. He and Ricardo had never been close. Both of them born to a father half Mexican and half Irish, and a mother whose paternal side was Irish and maternal side Hopi Indian, they had differed substantially in interests as well as looks.

Martin Dimas had made a name for himself as a trapper in the mountains. He made infrequent trips back, but never stayed long enough to get to know his sons.

Dark-skinned Ricardo brooded over his older brother's lighter skin and ease at making friends, while his older brother piled resentment and guilt one upon the other for not being able to keep either his mother or his younger brother happy as they struggled to survive on a small farm along the Missouri River.

Dimas had decided he had done what he could, always, to make things better between them. As the eldest, he had been responsible for setting examples. But why didn't Ricardo respond to them? Maybe he should have been more forceful with his brother, pushed him harder to make something of himself and to stay out of trouble. God knows he did everything short of tying his brother up and keeping close watch over him.

Most of their troubles, he had concluded, were not for want of food and clothing. He had learned a lot about survival during his mountain-man father's short stays at home, becoming an astute student capable of emulating everything his father taught him within a short period of time. The ways of trapping and hunting had brought needed food and income for the household.

Ricardo had refused to join them, preferring to take his rebellion into St. Louis, where he might find other young men with equal bitterness. Together they had formed gangs and terrorized older parts of the city.

Dimas found it hard to understand why his father showed so much apathy toward Ricardo's insolence. That Ricardo shunned him seemed not to matter. He had taken no offense, merely saying, "John, you and he are different, and it's nothing to worry about. If he wants, some time when he is ready, you can teach him what I'm teaching you."

"I believe he's learning what he wants to learn from others who think like him," Dimas had countered. "I see it as dangerous."

With a shrug, his father had always ended it. "You have your own plate full, don't you?"

With that in mind, Dimas had left Ricardo to his own devices. His father had left for the mountains for good when he was eighteen and Ricardo fourteen. They had never seen him again.

At the age of twenty-one, Dimas had traveled first to Taos and then farther north, well into the Rocky Mountains, nearly to the Canadian border. From there he had turned an about-face, clear back down to the Nueces River, where he had fought with the Texans against Mexico.

After the war, he had searched long and hard for his father, to no avail. He had wanted to express anger to his father for staying away so long and to tell him that Ricardo had left home and that their mother was slowly dying of consumption. "Likely dying of a broken heart," he had wanted to say. "The disease is just the manifestation of it."

In all the searching Dimas had learned where his father had been but had never caught up to him. Indians and traders alike knew him and had their own stories, and they had all agreed he was a mysterious and unpredictable man. "In some ways," one of them had said, "you seem to be just like him."

In looking at the children who had arrived at the boardinghouse, Dimas could see the same angry faces on some of the boys as he had on Ricardo, and the look of frustration and entrapment in their eyes. They had no place to go and nothing to look forward to.

Elisa's two boys, though fatherless, at least had a mother who put their needs ahead of her own, and a grandfather they could speak of with pride. Francis, having just turned seven, was slow to comment, while Manuel made his eager nature known to one and all.

Just five, he believed he could rope any tiger within roping distance any time he wished.

While Francis and the rest of the children decided to pay attention to a stray puppy that had wandered by, Manuel took Dimas aside to reveal a secret.

"There's something maybe you don't know about me," he said with a sly smile.

"What's that?" Dimas asked.

Manuel smiled. "I am an outlaw sometimes myself."

"How so, Manuel?"

"Sometimes my mother gets angry at the things I do and I go to my hideout."

"You have a hideout?"

"Yes, I do. Do you want to see it?"

"I would like that, Manuel. It will be our secret."

Manuel led Dimas outside through the back door and to a spot along the side of the house, in the shade under a paloverde tree. "It's back there," he whispered.

Dimas followed Manuel behind a large shrub beside the house. Manuel pulled a loose board from the side of the building and pointed.

"See? We used to have a very big dog and she dug a hole under there to have puppies in. She just kept digging and digging. I thought she wasn't going to be finished digging—ever!"

"It's a large hole, Manuel," Dimas agreed. "A very good place to hide."

"Mama never finds me here. Not even Francis. Nobody."

"It's a pretty good secret you have here, Manuel. I am glad you showed it to me." He took the boy gently by both shoulders. "I'm going to ask something of you, Manuel. I'm going to ask if you will share this hideout with me, if I ever need it."

Manuel smiled broadly. "Yes, of course."

"But you can't tell anyone that you're sharing it with me, do you understand?"

Manuel turned serious. "No one at all?"

"No one, Manuel. That's because if someone comes to look for me and I have to hide from them, no one at all must know I'm here. Do you understand that?"

"What if they ask me?"

"If anyone comes looking for me, and I'm gone, you just go somewhere else and stay away from them, so they won't ask you. Can you do that?"

Manuel frowned.

"It may never happen that I need to go here to hide," Dimas explained. "But if I am to ride with Joaquín, I have to stay away from some men who don't like either of us. Like those men from this morning, and last night."

Manuel nodded. "I understand, I think."

"This is how it is," Dimas explained further. "If Joaquín was here and men came to look for him, you wouldn't want them to find him, would you?"

"No, not at all."

"Think of it that way, then. Okay?"

"I will, Señor Dimas. You can count on me."

Maura sat beside Trenton Sterns at Don Luis Markham's holiday table. Sterns had been seated at Markham's right hand, and Maura beside him. Various dignitaries completed the ensemble around the long redwood table, including a state representative and two senatorial hopefuls from Sacramento. Maura had never seen either of them before, and Sterns didn't know them personally, only that they had an alliance with Markham of some kind.

They had arrived the night before and were, for the most part, hung over from the fandango that Don Luis had thrown in their honor. Markham had taken delivery of a dozen additional women to complement those he already kept. They were a mix of racial backgrounds, including Chinese and Anglo prostitutes from San Francisco, paid highly to be in attendance. Maura could hear them giggling and laughing while they waited for their food in an adjoining room.

The servants brought fried beef with peppers and

tamales and tortillas, along with assorted fruits and vegetable dishes. Maura couldn't keep track of it all and didn't care anyway. Her mind roamed outside the dining hall; past the headquarters grounds, to the open country along the coastline.

She had learned to ride on her uncle's estate and had always had a good rapport with horses of all kinds. Don Luis's Spanish mustangs held the kind of pride and stature she liked. If she could find a way to approach and saddle one of them, Trenton Sterns would never see her again.

Maura took a few bites of food and leaned slightly away from Sterns as he moved his face toward hers.

"Enjoying yourself, my dear?" he asked.

"The food is very good," she replied. "I just need to be allowed to eat it."

Sterns had every reason now to be cautious, both in word and action. He realized that his outburst the night of the raid in Los Angeles had alienated her completely and that in so many ways she was telling him their relationship was over. She refused to allow him into her room and no matter what he said and did for her now, she wouldn't respond. It troubled him deeply, as he couldn't allow her to get away. He needed Maura Walsh. The marriage had to take place as soon as possible.

For that to happen, he would be forced to spend

time and money winning back her affections. He had to regain her trust and make her believe that he had never meant what he said to her, that the stress of the made up raid and the seriousness of Joaquín Murrieta had weighed so heavily on his mind that he had not been himself. He believed it could work; he just needed an infallible way to get it done.

He determined the orphanage to be the key. He brought it up to her incessantly, promising that they would look at the boardinghouse tomorrow, and meet with the young Mexican woman who lived there, daughter to the old man Markham hated so badly and was so determined to locate.

As the meal continued, Markham saluted his friends. He emphasized that the roadways were treacherous and that he could make traveling safe once again if the California government desired that to be so. "I can place men to guard special coaches and to assist travelers of esteem, if that is required."

The political guests grunted their approval and raised large glasses of wine. One of them said to Maura, "You would appreciate being cared for well while on the trail, wouldn't you?"

"Does your wife appreciate being cared for?" Maura asked him. He hesitated and she added, "Why didn't you bring her along?"

The politician looked to Markham. The *ranchero*

saw that his friend needed help and said, "His wife, as well as the other wives, are home taking care of their families. Some day you will have a family and then you will know where you must be."

"No one need tell me where I must be, Don Luis," Maura told him. "A husband who cares will be sure to take me and the family along."

Everyone was silent, even the women in the other room. Two of them stuck their heads around the corner, and Markham frowned at them.

Maura scooted her chair back. "If you will excuse me, gentlemen."

She got up and hurried from the room. Sterns set his glass down and rose from his seat.

"I don't think she feels all that well," he said.

Maura stood on the veranda, peering out over the ocean. Sterns eased up beside her. He leaned over and whispered into Maura's ear.

"I can get us away from here, Maura. It will be just the two of us."

"You can do that, Trent?"

"Certainly, Maura. We'll have a bountiful life together, you and I, if you say yes to the marriage."

"I already have a bountiful life, Trent. I don't need to marry you for that."

"I don't know what to say. Lord knows I've apologized enough, I would think."

"Nothing is the same, Trent," she said. "I can't see how it ever will be again."

"It can be, Maura, if you'll only allow it."

"I see you differently now, that's all. I don't see you as someone I want to marry anymore."

"I have a surprise for you," Sterns said. "Let's go into town and see what that boardinghouse looks like—see if it's something that will suit you as an orphanage. What do you say?"

"When?"

"Right now. We have plenty of time."

Maura thought a moment. "What about Don Luis and his guests?"

"He told me earlier today that I could have the next few days off, so we could spend some time together. This is the best way I know how to do it. Except, of course, making you my bride. We could get the orphanage situation taken care of and set the wedding for Sunday. What do you say, Maura? It would make me so very happy. And you, too. You know that we still have something." He couldn't stand Maura's silence and added, "I'm saying that if you like the facilities, we can proceed and pretend the other night never happened."

Maura was still thinking. "Slow yourself down, Trent. One thing at a time."

"Do you feel like a ride into town? Right away? To meet with the young woman?"

"Are you sure she's there?"

"Where else would she be? I'll let Don Luis know we're leaving."

Maura walked farther on the veranda, taking in the view, while Sterns hurried toward the door. He discovered Markham just inside, waiting for him, smoking a cigarillo. The guests had adjourned to the other room, where the ladies were waiting for them.

"A little talk with Maura? Did it help?" he asked Sterns.

"Yes, things are fine."

"What is it you've planned?" he asked Sterns.

"Planned?"

"Listen, I know how you seek to please her. What is it you'll do for her?"

"She wishes to go into town and see the boarding-house that could become the orphanage," Sterns replied.

"Oh, yes. She has a dream of caring for many children. That's right."

"She insists on going now."

Markham frowned. "She doesn't care for my guests, that I know. But to be so rude as to just leave?"

"I think she's just anxious to get things moving, is all. You can see how that would be important to her, don't you?"

Markham studied him. "I see. She is a headstrong one, isn't she?"

"Yes, she is."

"Aha!" Markham clapped him hard on the shoulder. "Just the kind of woman we need around here, eh? I love the challenge of that kind of woman." His eyes became dark. "You see, my good man, a headstrong woman is like a headstrong horse. They make it difficult for you to ride them."

Sterns tried to smile.

"But that's a good thing. No? A good horse is a challenge, and one worth winning."

Sterns shifted his feet. "I have the upper hand with her, Don Luis."

"I'm sure that you do, Trent. But if you ever need any help, with the breaking or riding." He laughed. "Go ahead and take her into town. I'll send some of the men with you?"

"Why do we need anyone with us, Don Luis?"

Markham blew a cloud of smoke. "Because I still want to talk to that *pistolero*, John Dimas, that's why. Maybe he's still there. No?"

"I don't know."

"I know that he is. I've had some men watching. The padres are gone and he hasn't left."

"Do we have to look for John Dimas right now?"

"You know what's most important to me, Trent, don't you?"

Sterns nodded. "We'll look at the property and bring the *pistolero* back to you."

"Yes, you will do that." Markham ground his cigarillo out under his bootheel. "Last time I sent you on a mission, you failed me. Don't ever let that happen again."

Sterns felt his stomach tighten.

"Do you understand me?" Markham pressed.

"Perfectly, Don Luis."

"Good. Get to it, then."

With a thin smile Markham turned back inside to join the others. His spurs jingled loudly as he clomped inside.

Sterns hurried back to Maura. She stood facing the ocean, watching a herd of mustangs race along the edge of a cliff, with the endless water rolling behind them.

"Aren't they beautiful?" she said. "So wild and free."

"They are," he said flatly. "Are you ready to go?"

"Right now?"

"That's what I said, Maura. You've put me in a hard place, and I hope you're content with it."

EIGHT

The meal was finished and everyone had eaten their fill of chicken and duck, all roasted inside a small oven in the yard behind the kitchen. Women of the community had donated everything. Upon hearing about the orphans, they had brought food and clothing to help out.

Elisa and two Mexican women had spent the morning making tortillas and tamales. Some dried peppers, brought with the other provisions and soaked in water before frying, had rounded out the meal.

The children focused their attention at play in and around the building. They had finally lost their continuous fixation on Dimas. He was still a very interesting person, but in their minds there was little left to learn about him.

Since leaving, the two Franciscans had returned

once with the women who had brought the provisions, to bless the meal. They had decided to assist with the parish church, as the fall festivity season was a very busy time. They promised to drop by on occasion to see how things were going.

Somewhat overcome with all the attention at first, Elisa had adjusted to the change. Her interest in helping other children besides her own had come to fruition very quickly.

Dimas had spent considerable time asking her about her father and where he might have gone. Neither she nor the two boys seemed particularly disturbed about the fact that he still hadn't come back. "He'll show up in his own time," she had remarked to Dimas. "No need to worry about him."

While the children played outside, he talked to Elisa again while she sewed a hem into a colorful dress.

"Surely you must have some idea about your father," Dimas persisted. "Where's he at now?"

"Far away from Don Luis Markham." After a silence, she added, "That man is trying to pay off too many powerful people, so that he can keep his hacienda."

"I'm asking you if he doesn't send people around to give you information so that you won't worry about him," Dimas persisted.

"He sees a lot of the other Californios losing their grants, being kicked off the land. He will stop at nothing to line the pockets of those in power and build his own wealth as well."

"Like one of those women who brought the food the other day," Dimas said. "She whispered to you for a long time."

Elisa smiled. "Maybe she wanted to know how well I know you."

"I doubt it."

"And if I didn't know you that way, would I mind if she did." She began to laugh.

"You're just trying to throw me off," Dimas said.

"You're right. She didn't say that. Her name is Carlotta, and she does have an interest in your well-being, though."

Dimas continued to press her. "At times like this, where has your father gone before?"

"He never tells me. Why should he?"

"You're his daughter."

"He doesn't want to endanger me, Señor Dimas. He wouldn't have come here this time if he hadn't been worried about Manuel."

She explained that Manuel had been sick, but with a dose of herbs that one of the women had given him, he had recovered totally.

"You have to understand," Elisa explained. "My father is different. He can see things. He knows things. Do you understand me?"

"Yes, I believe so," Dimas replied.

"It's a gift that he has," she continued.

"I understand," Dimas said. "I was hoping to be able to talk to him again."

She turned from her sewing. "You will talk to him again, Señor Dimas. When the time is right. But you can't push it."

Dimas knew she would provide the information he needed in her own good time. But his time was growing short. He had decided that Percival was the key link in finding his brother, Ricardo, and he needed to find the old man as quickly as possible.

She resumed her work. "Maybe now you can see how strange life is at times. He finds you on the beach and you find him and bring him here. The men come, and if you hadn't been here, things would have ended very differently." She looked into his eyes. "You don't have to worry about it. They made you do it. You will not be haunted by their spirits." She went back to her sewing.

Dimas started in again. "He left his cane." He had found the walking stick lying under the table the night of the attack.

"He has others."

"Perhaps, but this one seemed special to him."

"Maybe he wants you to take it to him," Elisa suggested. "When he calls you to bring it to him."

Manuel suddenly burst through the door to announce that riders were approaching. "Some of the same men who were here the other day," he gasped. "This time they have a woman with them."

Dimas looked out a window and saw that Maura Walsh rode with Sterns and a number of Markham's men.

"They've come for you, again, haven't they?" Elisa said.

"I'm going out the back door," Dimas said. "If the ask, just tell them I'm gone. For all practical purposes, I am."

As Maura dismounted, she noted fear in the eyes of the young Mexican woman, who introduced herself as Elisa. Sterns and the others walked past her and the children, some of them entering the house while others circled the perimeter.

"Please excuse us, Señorita," Sterns said. "We're hunting outlaws."

"There are no outlaws here," Elisa told him.

"I hope not," Stern's said. He turned to Maura. "Keep yourself busy with her."

"I don't mean to intrude," Maura said. "It was not my idea to have all these men along."

"I understand," she said. "I'm always glad to have visitors. Have some holiday food if you want."

The children followed Elisa inside like a clutch of small chicks. They huddled themselves around her, their large round eyes wet with fear, while Sterns yelled orders to the men as they combed the building, room by room.

"Thank you, we ate," Maura said. "Really, I have no idea what's going on."

"They say they look for outlaws but they are the robbers and thieves," Elisa blurted. "They are brutal and don't care about anything or anyone."

Maura hurried after Sterns and stopped him. "You told me we were coming here to talk to her about making this place an orphanage."

"There are dangerous men about, Maura," Sterns insisted. "We have reason to believe one or more of them could be in hiding here."

Maura returned to the kitchen. "Who are they looking for?" she asked. She noticed the young woman's two sons suddenly look up at her.

"Who can say what they're doing?" Elisa replied. "Probably looking for gold, thinking there is some stashed. Did you know that some Yankees tore apart the floor of one of the old missions looking for hidden treasure? Just tore everything up. Someone saw gold flakes on the roots of an onion they pulled from the garden. So they thought there must be bags of nuggets hidden everywhere."

Maura stared at her. "You surely don't have gold here."

"Do I look to you to be rich, Señorita?" Elisa suddenly bowed. "My apologies for saying such rude things to you."

"I'm not offended," Maura told her. "I wouldn't want a bunch of men searching through my home, either. Let me tell them to stop."

"Don't bother. They won't listen to you."

"They will listen to me. Their leader is my fiancé."

"I see." Elisa studied her. "If you don't approve of what they're doing, then why did you come?"

"Not to look for outlaws, or for gold, or any other reason such as that," Maura replied. "I've been told that you have been considering using this as an orphanage. I can see that there are a number of children here, already."

"It's not a large place," Elisa said. "I can't take care of very many."

"I've come to ask if you'd like to maybe expand, build on to your existing residence, so that there would be more room."

Elisa seemed stunned. "Who would do this?"

"I would see to it. I would finance you, if you wanted that."

"But why?"

"Why not?" Maura asked. "When I was young, I was orphaned for a time. I was lucky and was discovered by family, and have done very well in life. Why not share that good fortune, if I can?"

"Don Luis Markham told you to do this?"

"Don Luis Markham has nothing to do with it," Maura said forcefully. "This is my own idea, and I just wanted to see if it was something that might interest you. Perhaps I'm wasting your time and mine, both."

"Oh, no. Please!" Elisa made the sign of the cross over herself. "The Blessed Virgin has smiled down upon me. Where did She find you, to bring you here?"

As the women talked, Manuel grew more restless. He was concerned that Señor Dimas had become too frightened to stay put in the hideout, that he had somehow decided to escape into the open if he could and try to get away from these bad men.

Manuel didn't want that at all. He wanted Señor Dimas to stay hidden, to remain safe in the dark hole where no one would find him. It was the best place to be—the only place to be. He had to check on Señor

Dimas and tell him to just stay put and not be afraid, before it was too late.

He eased away from his mother and then outside. Francis watched him but said nothing.

As Manuel rounded the corner of the building, he noticed a man just off to hís left, just standing near a paloverde, watching intently. It was too late to warn Señor Dimas. The man must surely be just waiting for him to leave the hideaway.

But the man wasn't watching the building, where the hideaway was located, behind the big bush. Manuel knew that instead, the man was watching him.

The man began to laugh. Manuel turned and began to run. But the man was upon him. He grabbed him by the hair and jerked his head back, laughing even harder.

From where he hid, Dimas heard Manuel's cries. The coarseness of the man's voice as he interrogated the small boy grated heavily on his nerves. He cracked open the board to listen.

Manuel was crying. He pleaded for the man to stop.

"You must know where the *pistolero* is, eh? Tell me or I'll pull harder."

Dimas burst from the hideaway, past the shrub and out into the open. He had come so fast that the outlaw hadn't time to fully realize it until Dimas was nearly upon him.

With a laugh, the outlaw reacted quickly, pulling a knife. He held it against Manuel's throat.

"Ah! *Pistolero!* You don't want me to do this to him, do you?"

Dimas had little time to act. Already Sterns and the others were converging.

Dimas raised his left arm and pointed to nowhere in particular. A diversion. Just enough to cause the outlaw to avert his eyes. Just for a moment.

He did. There was just enough time.

Dimas brought his pistol out and fired. The ball entered the outlaw's face through his upper lip, just under the nose, shattering the inside of his mouth and fragmenting back into his brain. He spun, the knife flying from his hand, and slammed into the tree on his way down.

Sterns and the others were there, guns ready.

"Don't shoot him!" Sterns roared.

Dimas felt his pistol slip from his grip as Sterns grabbed it. Another outlaw, screaming in Spanish, knelt beside the fallen one, trying to stop him from flipping and flopping.

Dimas noticed Maura Walsh running out of the building. Elisa followed right behind her, yelling, "Manuel! Manuel!"

Maura stopped and stared. Elisa was crying, holding Manuel close to her side.

"Trent, what is all this about?" she asked.

"You have to stay out of this, Maura. I mean it!" He turned to Dimas and pointed to the fallen man. "Foolish thing to do," he said.

The outlaw screaming in Spanish suddenly rose to his feet and crashed past Sterns, his revolver raised. He brought it down hard. Dimas managed to raise his arm in time. The barrel glanced off his wrist, but then slammed into his throat.

Dimas fell to his knees, clutching his Adam's apple. His wrist felt numb but the pain in his throat was like fire. He wanted to vomit, but held it back.

Subdued by the others, the screaming outlaw was hauled away. Sterns knelt down beside Dimas and said, "You shot his brother, one of Markham's best men. You'll pay dearly for it."

Markham's men hauled Dimas to his feet and bound his wrists tightly behind his back. One of them pulled a heavy knit cloth bag down over his head, blinding him. Dimas struggled to stay on his feet.

Maura stepped forward. "You haven't yet told me what he's done, Trent."

"You just saw him shoot a man in cold blood."

"Not a man, Trent. Only something far lower than an animal would put a knife to a small boy's throat."

From nearby Dimas heard a taunting voice as one of Markham's men spoke to the group.

"Can you see this Yankee gringo when Don Luis puts those things on him?" one of them said to the others. They all laughed. "Crawling and biting? I hope we can watch." More laughter.

"That's enough," Sterns told them. "We got what we came for. Mount up."

The children had all gathered around Elisa, many of them weeping openly. Especially Manuel, who sobbed into his mother's skirt.

"I don't understand any of this, Trent," Maura said.

Sterns took her aside. "This man is not the knight in shining armor that you'd have me believe. He helped Joaquín Murrieta rob the town the other night. He's a killer, Maura. We're going to see that he doesn't do any more of it."

"How can you be so certain of that?"

"Don Luis Markham makes it his business to know who the enemy is," Sterns replied.

Maura backed away from him. "I'm not certain I want to return to the ranch," she said.

"I wish you would understand," Sterns pleaded. "It's all for your safety. If there are men like this one here, how can it ever be safe for children?"

"I'll go back with you for now," Maura said. "But we have an awful lot of things to discuss."

Dimas sat bound in a half-lit room somewhere within the ranch headquarters. They had ripped his shirt off and tied him to a wooden chair, placing him with the back of the chair against his chest, to keep his shoulders and back exposed. They had bound his wrists behind him and secured his lower legs to the chair legs. To keep him as secure as possible, they had also looped another small rope around his neck and through the spokes of the chair's back.

His face was wet with sweat inside the heavy cloth covering over his head. He struggled to breathe. His throat had nearly swollen shut and his vocal cords, where the pistol barrel had struck, felt like a lump of rock in his neck.

He felt rough hands as they started to pull the cloth from his head.

"No, don't remove it," Markham ordered. "It's better done this way."

Dimas wondered if his day to die had finally come. The smell told him that the room was a place of blood, where much of it had been spilled and left to dry. He could feel heat off to his left and knew it came from a stove of some kind.

In a low voice, Markham said to one of his men, "Add a little more wood, Bestez."

Dimas struggled to bring himself upright, but was secured too tightly.

"You should relax," Markham told him. "Enjoy your stay." He lit a cigarillo and began to walk a circle around him. "I realize that you are at a disadvantage with your speech at this time," he said. "That is unfortunate. I have much that I want to hear from you. Can you say anything at all?"

Dimas shook his head no.

Markham nodded to Bestez, who stood behind Dimas. Bestez abruptly struck him across his bare back with a horsewhip. Dimas groaned.

"Your name."

Dimas spoke hoarsely, the pain cutting off his words. The horsewhip came down on his back again.

"Yes, it is difficult, but you must exert yourself," Markham said. He blew smoke from his cigarillo. "Try again."

Dimas let out a hoarse whisper and tensed, waiting for the whip to fall. Markham had his hand raised. As soon as Dimas eased up a bit, the whip came down again.

"This hitting in the throat with a gun barrel, it should never have happened to you," Markham said. "I have taken care of the man who did it. Ill-advised of him, wouldn't you say?"

Bestez opened a door. From outside came the distinctive crack of a bullwhip, followed by the wails of a man in great pain.

"If he survives his punishment," Markham added, "he will be placed as a slave along with my Indians. That is, if he survives. He did not behave well in front of women and children. Nor did his brother. But then, you took care of that matter, didn't you?"

Dimas groaned.

"I didn't hear you," Markham said.

The whip didn't come down. "Yes," Dimas managed.

"Oh, I can see how it pains you to talk," Markham said. "For the time being, nod yes or shake you head no. Do you understand?"

Dimas nodded that he understood.

"Good," Markham said. "Now, I want you to try very hard to understand some things. We'll get started."

NINE

Markham paced for a moment.

"When my men brought you here, did they take you to a place overlooking the ocean?" When Dimas nodded, he added, "And when they took the cloth off your head, did you note how beautiful it was, and how the cattle and the horses love to graze in the swamp grass at the mouth of the big stream that angles down from the mountains? Did you?"

Dimas nodded.

"This land, this hacienda, has been in my family for three generations, Señor Dimas. If you were me, would you give all that up?"

Dimas shook his head no. The whip came down.

"I don't believe you, Mr. *Pistolero*. Maybe you have Spanish blood, maybe some Indian blood as well, but you are mostly Yankee. And it is the Yankees who have this land now to call their own. But not my land! Do you understand?"

Dimas nodded and waited for the whip from Bestez. Instead Bestez snapped it past his ear and chuckled.

"Do you know this old man, Percival?"

Dimas shook his head yes.

"Do you know where he is at this time?"

Dimas shook his head no. Bestez struck again, this time across the back of his neck.

"Do you know where he is at this time?"

Again, Dimas shook his head no and tensed, awaiting the pain. Markham kept his hand raised.

"Listen," Markham said at length, "I think I believe you. Should I believe you?"

Dimas nodded yes. Markham lowered his hand and the whip came down across Dimas's left arm. He held his breath to try to combat the agony. The whip strokes were vicious, but still couldn't compare to the throbbing in his throat.

Dimas felt the ropes securing him to the chair loosen. First his legs and then the one around his neck.

"I want you to turn around and sit up in the chair, Señor Dimas. Do you understand?"

Dimas nodded, but was slow to move. The whip came down hard across his back. He arched himself up and quickly turned and rose to his feet. He kicked out with all his might. The blow struck Bestez's right knee. He heard the man's kneecap crack like a sharp stick.

Bestez dropped to the floor, yelling. Dimas kicked out again, smashing his face. Markham brought the butt end of the whip down across Dima's head.

Markham called two other men who quickly tied him to the chair, facing out. The wraps around him were so tight he could barely breathe. Coupled with his swollen throat, he grew close to passing out.

"Loosen the ropes a little," Markham ordered. "He needs to be able to scream, if he feels like it."

Dimas felt the ropes ease their grip. The men were rough, slamming him in the throat as often as they could. He kept his chin lowered, but the swelling prohibited him from protecting his Adam's apple at all.

Finally, they moved away from him.

"Bring me the box," Markham said.

"Let me help," Bestez insisted.

Dimas tightened. He knew the box held something he didn't want to know about, something that would, as they had said laughingly at the boardinghouse, crawl on him and bite him.

"Here's what I'm going to do, Señor Dimas," Markham said. "I'm going to introduce you to one of my good friends. He lives in the desert to the north. He has been brought here to visit."

Dimas felt the back of Markham's hand on his stomach, followed by eight hairy legs that sat still for a moment, and then began to move slowly up his chest. He didn't need eyes to realize that Markham had placed a tarantula on him.

"You see, there is nothing to be afraid of, Señor Dimas," Markham said. "A gentle creature. Can you see that?"

Dimas sat very still. The hairy legs made their way slowly toward his neck. He felt Markham's hand again, and the spider was gone. Then, through his pain, he heard Bestez chuckle quietly.

"I know that you and the old man, Percival, have become good friends," Markham continued. "But that old man is no friend of mine. I won't go into particulars, but you should know that he cannot stay alive. So, I want to teach you something right now."

Again Bestez chuckled.

"Hand me the pan," Markham said to him. "And the lid."

Dimas felt the heat of the frying pan close to his chest. He could hear the large spider thumping around underneath, trying to get out.

"You see, Señor Dimas," Markham said, "even when a normally gentle creature becomes angered, 'heated,' so to speak, it can become very unpleasant. Here, I will show you."

Dimas tried to rise up but the two men held his shoulders, forcing him back down. He gritted his teeth and listened to Bestez laugh.

Markham flipped the angry spider out of the pan and squarely onto Dimas's chest. The bite felt like two sharp needles penetrating clear through his skin. The spider hung tightly until Markham brushed it off and shot it as it hit the floor.

"There, now you understand," Markham told Dimas. "There are things I need to know from you and I get heated when you don't tell me."

Dimas sat very still. Bestez roughly removed the head covering and Dimas blinked. When he could see, he looked at his chest. Two fang holes ran with trickles of blood. Swelling had already begun.

"Don't worry, you won't die, Señor Dimas," Markham promised. "You will be uncomfortable for a time, perhaps. But you'll live to tell me what I want to know. Adios for now, my friend."

Maura stood on the veranda, looking out across the ocean. The moon hung low over the water and the waves lapped the shore with tops that shone white and frothy. In the distance a few nightbirds cried. Along the shore, late evening gulls hovered over the beach, watching for whatever meal the surf might bring in.

She looked back over her shoulder. Inside, Sterns and Don Luis discussed something. Sterns had his arms crossed, scowling at the floor. They had been at it for a full half hour. In the other room, the lady guests entertained the men. They whirled and twirled in colored skirts while the men laughed and threw coins at them.

Maura wanted something cleared up—something about travel north by land, to drive a herd of horses somewhere to sell. She knew that Markham meant to send her fiancé along with the vaqueros, supposedly because the politicians would be going along as well. Apparently they needed babysitting until they got back to San Francisco. They wanted to see the gold camps along the way, and Markham didn't want them getting into trouble at some fandango.

"If some of those Mexican women in the camps knew who they were," Sterns had remarked, "their entrails would color the barroom floor."

An interesting thought that Maura had pondered, considering that the women now entertaining them would likely be equally happy to do it.

When Sterns had told her he would be required to accompany them, she had told him if he went, so would she. His expression had revealed the tremendous stress he felt. Inside, he still held much of what she had first seen in him, but Markham's influence was proving to be much too strong.

Maura continued to watch inside. The women stepped up their dancing tempo and began to remove their skirts and tops. Some danced naked, others scantily clad. Sterns didn't go into the room with Markham to join the other men, to grope and be groped. Instead, he watched from the doorway, turning his head back every now and then to look at Maura.

She turned and began to walk along the veranda, away from the main door. Sterns finally came out and, after finding her, asked, "Why are you up so late?"

"You've been avoiding the discussion we need to have," she told him.

"You know that I've been arguing against going up north," he said. "I've fought it hard. But when Don Luis Markham wants something, he gets it."

"What does he want, exactly?" Maura asked.

"He wants me to go, and for you to stay here."

"And how do you feel about that, Trent?"

"He's the boss, Maura. I can't buck him."

"You can't buck him? Even after what I told you?"

Sterns paced for a time. "Maybe we should get married before I leave."

Maura laughed. "Do you think that would stop him?"

"What do you suggest?"

"At least you're as certain as I am of his intentions."

She waited for a reaction. "Go back inside and tell him that I'm going north with you."

"Do you really think that's wise?"

"What will he do to me? Torture me, like he did John Dimas?" She paused. "Is he dead?"

"No, but he wishes he was, I'm sure. What do you care about him?"

"The point is, Markham has overstepped his bounds, and he'll come to answer for it. Why do you want to be part of that?"

Stern paced. "Okay, he gave me a little section of the ranch, in exchange for my connections in San Francisco and Sacramento."

"A little section to you is a huge section to him."

"I did it for us, Maura."

"Did we discuss it, Trent, living with Don Luis Markham looking in our windows?"

"That's not fair, Maura."

"He's no big brotherly type, Trent. Or haven't you noticed?" It was her turn to pace. "I don't know you anymore. You've become so wrapped up trying to please Markham that you've lost sight of everything else."

"I intend to become somebody, Maura," Sterns said. "My father never believed I could do that, could make my own mark in politics. He got help from my mother's side of the family. I'm never going to get any help from anyone, so I'm going it alone."

"But you're doing it at my expense. At our expense. Don't you see that?"

"I've got to get back to the party," he replied. "We'll talk more about this later."

Maura grabbed his arm. "Just remember this: If you go and leave me here, you'll come back and find me gone. I swear to God, Trent."

Sterns pulled away from her and stormed back inside.

•

In the darkness Dimas could hear the rush of the surf to shore. He lay on his side, still bound to the chair. His thrashing to try and break loose had resulted in exhaustion and an uncomfortable position on the floor. He knew though that his comfort level now was high compared to what it would become when Markham returned.

His throat hadn't improved, and his chest burned in a large circular area where the angry tarantula had bitten him. His mind was clouded, but he didn't know if it was from the bite or the lack of food and water. He didn't know whether it was real or he was imagining it. He was certain he heard the door creak open.

"Be still! Don't say a word!"

A harsh whisper. A woman's voice. A knife sliced through the ropes. He sat up and rubbed his arms and legs to bring the circulation back.

"Hold still," the woman said. She placed a poultice of plants and mud against the spider bite. "This will help you."

"I have to go." Dimas started to rise but was too weak.

"Your throat is badly hurt."

"Who are you?" Dimas managed.

"My name is Carlotta. I'm Elisa's friend," she replied. "She told me you'd been taken by Don Luis's men. She thought they might have already killed you. Thank the Christ Jesús and the saints that I've found you alive."

"I don't understand," Dimas said. "How did you get out here?"

"You don't think I can ride better than you?" She handed him a small piece of dried chaparral root. "Chew on this. It will give you strength."

Dimas chewed and took water from a skin bag she handed him.

"You took a dangerous chance," he said.

"Maybe," Carlotta agreed, "but you see, this was a good time to come. They are all so busy with the politicians and the horse herd that is to go north that they don't watch for other things all that well." Then she added, "Besides, Markham is too high-minded to think he might be vulnerable."

"You know a lot about what's going on, don't you?"

"I have to. We all have to."

Dimas stood up. "I don't know how to thank you."

"Don't thank me. Just escape this evil place and find a way to bring Don Luis Markham to justice."

Carlotta had no sooner left than the door cracked open again. Dimas grabbed a piece of wood for a club and waited.

Maura eased her way inside. "John? Are you here?"

Dimas lowered the club. "They didn't invite me to the party up at the main house."

"Your voice. What happened?"

"It'll get better. Why did you put yourself at risk?"

Maura took him by the arm and led him out to where she had tethered a large black stallion. "We can't waste time talking."

"Where's your horse?"

"I'll leave by the front door. Markham can't afford to try and stop me."

"You don't know Markham."

"And you don't know me." After a moment, she asked, "Where will you go?"

"North to the mines, to find my brother. I still think you should come along with me."

"Persistence is not a virtue in this case, John."

Dimas rubbed his throat and took a deep breath. "You know that better than me, I guess." He struggled into the saddle.

"I'm glad to finally hear someone say they have confidence in me."

"I just don't understand why you wouldn't leave right now, too."

"Why do you believe you have to understand everything a person does?" she asked him. "Let me help you this time. Your turn comes later, and I'll hold you to that."

Dimas left in the night, careful to avoid the vaqueros tending the horses along the slopes above the ranch. But before long, as the moon rose, he discovered that a group of riders was close behind.

As the stallion stretched to full speed, Dimas hung on to the saddle horn and the horse's mane tightly. Lead balls whined past him, and the stallion began to lengthen the distance between them and their pursuers. A sudden hitch in the animal's gait told Dimas that the stallion had taken a round in the hip.

Dimas worked the horse toward a trail that led down to the beach. He had come a good distance from the ranch, to where he had arrived on shore after the shipwreck. He rode down the trail to the bottom and loosed the stallion. Along the top, the riders began their descent on horseback to find him.

Dimas studied the area. He spotted the row of rocks that jutted up out of the water just off the beach where he and Percival had sat next to a fire.

After a frantic search, he found the gun cache right where he had left it and threw rocks aside until he was able to tear the bag free. He pulled two Colt Dragoon revolvers from the collection and hurried to load them, ramming powder and ball into the cylinders, while the vaqueros rode within yards of him, cursing in the darkness as they searched the area. One of them pointed him out to the others and fired at Dimas.

The ball splintered against a rock near his arm. Dimas opened fire, dropping the vaquero from the saddle, and two others as the entire group then began shooting at him. The darkness came to life with flashes of burning powder and as Dimas moved one way and another, shooting with both hands, Markham's men spread in all directions along the beach.

Three of them lay still, and two others writhed and moaned as he reloaded the pistols. Just four vaqueros remained. They sat their horses nearby, discussing their chances.

Finally, they came at him, screaming in the darkness, their pistols raised. Dimas threw a large chunk of driftwood in front of the lead rider's horse and the animal bolted to one side, throwing its rider into the sand. The other three riders turned and heeled their horses back up off the beach.

Dimas spoke in Spanish as the vaquero rose to his feet, holding his badly broken left arm.

"Get on your horse and go with the others," Dimas advised.

"Just be good to me and shoot," the vaquero begged. "Don Luis will have me flogged until I die anyway."

"Why do you have to go back there?" Dimas asked.

The vaquero was slow to answer. Dimas realized that he was stalling while the other three came at him from behind.

He heard the horses close as he turned. Broken arm or no, the vaquero jumped him, working to ram a knife home. Dimas slammed a pistol butt into his face, knocking him back. He shot the man point-blank and turned his fire on the oncoming riders.

A ball entered his left leg, just above the knee, as he dropped two of them from the saddle. The third shot him in the right leg, in nearly the same place, and yelled in jubilation as Dimas dropped to the ground. The vaquero rode his horse in close and leaned over to fire. Dimas, on his back, shot both pistols into the man's exposed middle.

Between limping badly and crawling, Dimas managed to catch a stray horse. He felt relief that neither leg had any bone damage, but the left one bled far worse than the right. He loaded one of the saddlebags with leather bags filled with ball and powder. He stuffed the two Dragoons into his belt and struggled atop the horse.

In his mind, Elisa's boardinghouse rose just ahead. He had to keep in mind the concept that he had already arrived, or he knew he would never make it there.

Agnes Sterns eased quietly through the main house. The last thing she wanted was for Don Luis Markham to discover her. She hadn't been able to sleep.

Upon seeing a light under her son's bedroom door, she knocked gently.

"Mother, what in the world?"

"Quick! Let me in and keep your voice down."

"You've been drinking."

"And it's not doing one damn bit of good."

"When are you going to learn that you can't forget Father that way?"

"Trenton, when your father died, I never shed a tear," she said. She watched his face twist with shock. "You didn't, either, and you know it."

"I never thought I'd hear you say it, Mother."

"You need to listen more closely to me, Trenton,

especially now." She pulled him over into a corner and spoke softly. "I overheard Markham talking to one of his men in the courtyard. Did you know they were going to steal gold from the mining camps along the way?"

"You heard him say this?"

"Trenton, you didn't answer my question." She read his silence and added, "For the love of God, I can't believe you would work for a man such as that."

"It's not that simple."

"I know you, Trenton, and I know how badly you want to succeed. But doing it this way will not work, I can assure you."

"I thought you said we were going to keep our voices down."

"You are going to book me passage on the next steamer back to San Francisco. If you're smart, you'll book Maura as well. She's the best thing that ever happened to you and you're within a short inch of ruining it."

Sterns thought about it. He had told Maura she had to stay with him. Perhaps if she went back to San Francisco with his mother, and he reunited with her later, he could salvage their relationship.

He would feel safer, though, not sending them by boat.

"Maura and the Mexican lady, Elisa, have gotten to

be good friends," he told his mother. "I believe it would be best to have you both go to her boarding-house. Markham had me take his tithing, plus extra, to the church the other day, and I learned that the two padres who brought the children down are going back up with some of them, and others as well. There are too many orphans coming in to take care of at one place."

"So, there will be a group taking children north?"

"A large group, I would imagine—men and women working for dispensations from the Church, and for the good of the children. They will all accompany the padres."

"I can ride in a wagon as well as the next person," she said. "Maura will prefer a horse, I'm sure. And what are you going to do?"

"I'll go north with the horses and the politicians. I'll meet you back home. We can put this all behind us." He hugged his mother. "I know I'd rather have you and Maura with me, but it's too dangerous."

"Danger is danger," she said. "One if by land, two if by sea. Wasn't that the message?"

TEN

Maura returned to the main house, wondering about the shooting she had heard earlier, off in the distance, somewhere along the beach. When it ended, she had wondered who had survived and who hadn't. She told herself not to worry. John Dimas was a hard man to put down. Then she wondered how it had come to pass, in such a short time, that she had come to care about him and what his fortunes might be. She didn't like to see anyone in trouble, but there was something different about how she felt about John Dimas.

She stood on the veranda, listening to the ocean, wondering how she would put together her exit from Don Luis Markham and his hacienda. She decided that she would approach her fiancé one last time and see if he might have come to his senses. She had a feeling he had been thinking long and hard about what she had told him.

Then she smelled the distinct odor of cigarillo smoke.

"Alone again, it would seem. Señor Sterns does not take good care of you at all, does he?"

Maura turned and faced Markham. "I take care of myself, thank you."

"That you do, and very well, I must say," he responded. "You really don't need Trenton Sterns at all, do you? Have you been thinking about that?" Maura didn't respond, and he added, "Perhaps a man like me would be more to your liking."

"You don't think much of Trenton, do you?" Maura pointed out.

"He is, shall we say, limited in his abilities at times."

"So, why do you call him your right-hand man?"

"Shall we say, he once represented a certain amount of influence in my behalf. Now that is passed."

"It passed after you used him to make inroads with the political powers in the state capital. Is that what you mean?"

"He wasn't really that close to any of them."

"Just close enough."

"Everything occurs within a matter of degrees, Señorita. I know I don't have to tell you that." He took a long puff. "Since meeting you, my right-hand man has changed. His directions seem confused, shall we say. I know he sees a lot in you. And, I suppose, the reverse is true?"

Maura took time to answer. "I know that when I first met him, Trenton had a different attitude about what he wanted from life. He seemed more vivacious. Now he seems pressured and uncertain."

"I hope you don't consider my influence to be untoward."

"I make no judgments."

"You should have pursued politics, Miss Walsh. In my estimation, you have a great deal of potential. But not in conjunction with Trenton." He stomped out the butt of his cigarillo. "But we must give Señor Sterns the benefit of the doubt. He has an awful lot on his mind tonight." He studied her. "Someone helped the *pistolero* break free. Did you see anything?"

"I heard gunshots a moment ago," she replied. "I assumed it was merely your own men. They use their knives and guns against one another at times, I understand."

Markham grunted. "Some squabbling among virile men is to be expected, don't you think?"

"There seems to be a steady diet of it here."

"Steady compared to what, Señorita? Can you compare your lifestyle in San Francisco to your new experience out here?"

"I was told it would be similar. I suppose I should blame only myself for such naïveté."

"Ah, but you will adjust," Markham said. "The late night suits you, and there are no more prettier nights than on my hacienda."

"I have to tell you, Mr. Markham, that I believe I prefer the bay breezes to the north." She stepped away from him. "Well, as you pointed out, it is late. I do hope that you enjoy the night air."

Dimas rode into Los Angeles with the rising of the sun. A few dogs barked, and at the edge of town a rooster crowed.

He held fast to his horse in front of Elisa's boardinghouse, badly weakened from his leg wounds. Holiday decorations adorned the sides of the building, and a nearby Joshua tree.

Elisa and the boys came out, along with Carlotta. The two women helped him out of the saddle.

"First, you are bitten by a spider, and now there are bullet holes in both your legs?" Carlotta exclaimed. "Holy Mother preserve us!"

Dimas spoke in a gravelly voice. "It's not that bad."

He collapsed. The two women turned him onto his back and wiped his face with a wet cloth.

Francis and Manuel saw a more effective method of reviving him. They lugged a clay jar of water over and tipped it onto Dimas.

"Careful, boys," Elisa ordered. "Can't you hear him sputtering?"

"It's good for him," Manuel insisted.

Elisa shook her head. "Not all at once."

Elisa and Carlotta helped Dimas inside to a chair at the table, where a lantern flickered.

Dimas could barely hold his head up. "Really, it's not that bad," he repeated.

"I'll dress your wounds," Carlotta said. "You'll heal fine if you get rest."

"I haven't time for rest."

Carlotta threw up her hands. "Then go ahead and jump off a cliff, Señor Dimas. Perhaps you would make it happen more quickly if you just went to Markham's ranch."

"I don't want everyone here in jeopardy again. If Markham's men come back, who knows what they'll do this time."

"They won't come back," Elisa insisted.

"What makes you so sure?" Dimas asked.

"Because they wouldn't think you foolish enough to return here." She smiled. "You must be blessed by all the saints and angels to still be alive."

Carlotta said, "You need to eat something. And don't protest. We have to feed the children anyway."

Elisa set to preparing eggs and peppers, with tortillas. Some of the children had gathered to see what was happening, and Carlotta herded them back to their rooms. They pointed and exclaimed that the *pistolero,* who was a good man, had survived to ride with Joaquín.

"Go on with you to your rooms, and wait until we call you to eat," Carlotta told them. She turned to Dimas. "I'll go back out and tell the Indians who work for Markham that you've taken a trail south."

"Don't risk your life for me, Carlotta," Dimas told her.

"It's not only for you," she insisted.

Francis and Manuel approached Dimas and both hugged him. "I want to tell you that I'm very sorry," Manuel said. "It was me who caused those bad men to take you away."

Dimas took a long breath. His wounds throbbed and all he wanted to do was lie down.

"Listen, Manuel," he said, "you aren't to blame at all. Remember that, will you?"

Manuel nodded. "It's just that I was always worried about you."

Elisa arrived with a plate filled with food. "He insisted I keep a candle burning so that the Blessed Virgin would send you peace and light," she said. "It worked."

Manuel rubbed a tear from his cheek. "I didn't mean to have them catch you."

Dimas hugged him tight. "Manuel, you are a good, strong boy. You needn't worry any longer. I'm just fine and I will always be fine."

"He's right. You have enough concerns," Elisa added. "Like finding a way not to fight with your brother."

Dimas looked across the table, to the chair where Percival had sat that night not long before. He turned to Elisa.

"Has your father returned?"

"He has not." Her mood turned somber. "But he is okay. I know that much."

"Is the time right for me to find him?"

"No."

Carlotta stood beside Elisa. "You need to eat, Señor Dimas. You need to eat and then rest, for a good long time. That is, if you're serious about finding Joaquín Murrieta."

With his stomach full, Dimas accepted the offer for temporary reprieve at the boardinghouse. Elisa had convinced him by informing him that the two padres were due to arrive before long, to take the children back north with them. After that, it would be wise if he found sanctuary in the nearby mountains.

Dimas settled himself on a small grass cot just inside the main door, sitting up with his back against the wall. Walking was out of the question and had it not been for the strong herb tea he had drunk and the poultices Carlotta placed on his wounds, he doubted he would even be conscious.

After reading a chapter of *Gulliver's Travels,* he heard the sound of approaching horses. He pulled out his pistol and prepared himself for more problems.

Manuel ran up to him and pointed at the revolver. "You won't need that this time, Señor Dimas."

Maura Walsh rode into the yard and dismounted. She began a conversation with Elisa and Carlotta, and the two women led her inside.

"My God, John!" she said.

"I'll live," Dimas said. "Do Markham and Sterns know you're gone?"

"Trent is about ten minutes behind me, with his mother, in a carriage."

"Maybe he's changed his colors after all. Your hope won't go to waste."

"You don't know what my hope is."

"I know what it used to be," Dimas said.

"Maybe things have changed for you as well," she

suggested. "As for me, I'm going ahead with my plans to start orphanages in the mining camps."

Maura explained to Dimas that she and Mrs. Sterns had decided to travel back north with the convoy of priests and orphans and the others who would go with them. Sterns would travel with the politicians and the vaqueros, led by Bestez.

"I'll base my work out of San Francisco," she said.

"Elisa will be disappointed, but you can't stay here, I guess."

Maura looked into the distance. "A lot could be done here, it's true. Trent didn't tell me what he got himself into, though, or what Markham got him into."

"And Markham certainly wants to keep tithing to the Church," Dimas remarked. "So you're safe with the padres."

Sterns arrived with his mother. He helped her down from the carriage and took her bags to one of the wagons. She made her way over to Dimas.

"You interested in racing stagecoaches?"

Dimas smiled. "You can drive this time."

"I guess we're all a family of fugitives from Don Luis Markham," she commented. "We'd better stick together."

She joined the women in the kitchen, and Sterns stepped forward and cleared his throat.

"I wouldn't blame you if you hated me to the core,"

he remarked. "I can only say I'm sorry for being such a fool."

Dimas shook his hand. "I'll not hold it against you. What will you do once you get back to San Francisco?"

"I'll find something. I have connections outside of politics. Markham has used me as much as he cares to. He's got everything lined up the way he wants it. He's likely glad to be rid of me."

"You know an awful lot about him and how he runs his business practices."

"He's not as worried about me as he is about you and that old man. He sees me as someone who doesn't want to bring all that up and cast doubt on myself."

"Maybe he's right about that," Dimas agreed. "You would have considerable to lose in the end."

"But you and the old man wouldn't," Sterns suggested. "He definitely sees you two as people who could bring him down."

"I don't agree," Dimas responded. "He doesn't think anyone could bring him down."

"He is a powerful man with a lot of connections," Sterns conceded. "But there are some organized groups outside of the usual political circles who could do him a lot of damage."

"Joaquín Murrieta?"

"Him, and the gangs that operate under him. They see him as a sellout and a traitor to their people."

"That kind of hate burns deep," Dimas agreed. "I can see how your trip up with horses and politicians could prove very dangerous, as well as interesting. I'll bet Maura is definitely worried for you."

"She has her own concerns traveling with the padres and the children," he said. "Yes, she is worried, though. I am for her as well." He paused and added, "I think I've lost her. I really do."

Maura stood a distance away and watched Trenton Sterns talk with Dimas. She realized that her relationship with Sterns could never be the same. Despite his efforts to prove he now had her best interests at heart, she couldn't make herself believe him—not entirely, though it did seem he wanted to make total amends. Enough had happened, though, that kept her from opening up as she had at one time.

She felt torn about leaving the area and returning to San Francisco. She had developed a very good friendship with Elisa, and under different circumstances their combined efforts to turn the boardinghouse into an orphanage might have proven to be her first priority. It would be difficult to bid farewell.

She wouldn't rule anything out, though. Perhaps the day would arrive when she would return and they would progress again with the plans for an orphanage.

She wanted to say a few parting words to Trenton Sterns and waited until he had completed his conversation with Dimas before she approached him. With their relationship on hold at best, she had trouble deciding whether advice was a good way to leave things with him. She felt it best to address some issues, though. She did still hold his best interest at heart.

"I don't know what you want to say," Sterns said as they walked through the vineyard. "But I want to apologize again for all that's happened. Had I to do it all over again, it would be different, believe me."

"I think you should make a clean break while you have the chance," Maura told him. "You don't have to travel with Markham's political puppets."

"He's already paid me to take them up," Sterns said.

"Give him back his money," Maura suggested. "Tell him you're on your own now."

"They want someone along with them besides the vaqueros driving the horses," Sterns told her. "I guess they see me as their only link to genteel society on the trip up."

"Why do you think you owe him anything, Trent?"

"I told you, Markham has already paid me for the trip." He took a deep breath. "I doubt we could have ever seen eye to eye on most issues, could we have?"

"Likely not," Maura agreed. "I just don't understand why you don't want to make your trip back an easier one. You could even travel with us. That would please your mother."

"It would be too difficult, Maura, considering where you and I are at right now," he said. "Besides, riding with women and children and priests can cramp a man's style."

"I see," Maura said. "There's lots of interesting places to discover along the way, huh? I just hope you don't get too curious."

In a short time the two priests arrived with over a dozen more orphans and a contingent of people who had volunteered to help escort the children to an orphanage located in one of the mining towns to the north.

Dimas watched them assemble. Elisa and Carlotta had already packed what scant items of clothing each child possessed. Both women hugged and kissed each child in turn and loaded them into wagons. It was Father Francis who came to Dimas as they were about to leave.

"Some of the children want you to travel with us," he said. "I told them you were too badly injured. It's just as well that you are, you know."

"Did you give them a sermon and tell them I'm not the kind of person they should look up to?"

"They are children, Señor Dimas. They shouldn't

have to view blood and death or be with someone who makes it his life."

"Have you ever had to kill anyone, Padre?" Dimas asked.

"I'm the one who grants absolution, Señor Dimas."

"Who is in charge of your absolution?"

"Señor Dimas, as I said, it is not permissible to allow a *pistolero* to travel with children. Would you argue that?"

"It seems the point is moot, wouldn't you agree?" When the padre didn't answer, he added, "Even if I was healthy, I wouldn't put the children at risk."

"How will you find your brother?"

"Pray for me, Father. Pray that I find him."

"It's time to leave," Father Francis said. "We have a long way to go. I will pray that your life gets better for you, and your brother's as well."

Just before they departed, Maura came over and extended her hand. "It's been good knowing you, John."

Dimas felt strange. "You saying goodbye?"

"In your condition, you won't be able to travel until at least spring," she replied. "I'll be back in San Francisco by then."

"How can you be sure where you'll be, Maura?" he asked. "Did you think last year at this time that you would be standing here talking to me, or even be in Los Angeles?"

"A good point," she conceded. "Where will you be, until you're well enough to travel?"

"I'll find a safe hideout somewhere," he replied. "I'm good at that."

"Too bad that has to be your life."

"It's the hand I was dealt."

"You can be an impetuous cardplayer at times," she told him.

"It's him or me," Dimas responded.

"Is that how it has to be?"

"Yes, when you wear pistols."

"And what if you don't wear them? What if you never needed them again?"

"There're too many who know me who would like that," Dimas responded.

"That's just the way you like it, I'm sure. Are there times when you press it?" When he turned away she added, "I hope you heal quickly, and that you find your brother."

"I'm not certain at this point which one will be more difficult to accomplish."

Maura reached into her bag. "Hold out your hand, please." She placed the five-dollar gold piece into Dimas's palm. "For good luck," she said.

A dozen more travelers arrived for the trip. After the packing was ended and the wagons were lined up, they left with the sun shining in their faces. Some of the men drove a few steers alongside to feed the group, and a couple of milch cows. They sang Spanish songs as they disappeared into the distance.

"A long road ahead," Dimas said.

Elisa wiped away a tear. "I hope they all find happiness."

Carlotta stood with an arm around her. "They will be fine. Their journey is blessed," she said.

ELEVEN

Don Luis Markham stood on his veranda and smoked a cigarillo. The sun had just fallen into the ocean and its last rays lit the clouds in subtle reds and pinks.

The beauty was lost on him, for his smile came from other feelings inside. His efforts to secure the support of the right political circles looked to be a success, so his future, for the moment at least, seemed to be glowing. Certainly it would take more gold than he had anticipated, but there were a lot of sources from which to obtain it. If he could continue to keep his alliances strong, his hacienda would remain untouchable to those who wanted it for themselves.

Before the war and the loss of power to the United States, his own place had remained secure. His family's land grant had come through strong political ties to the Mexican government. His family had been affluent and respected. Now all that was past, and even though he maintained ties to former alliances, they had no effect in California any longer.

He had tried to make an impact on John Dimas, to allow him to understand why he must suffer punishment and why he could not live. Surely he understood this. After all, had he been in a similar position, wouldn't he be equally driven to keep what was rightly his? The mere fact that he had entered the situation not of his own accord did not matter. He had been in a certain place at a certain time, however unfortunate.

As he puffed, Markham thought about his family, or what used to be family. Everyone had deserted him, and painful as it was at the time, it now served him well. There was no one to have to consult on business matters and no one with whom to share the take.

Immediately before the war, when everyone had already known what the outcome would be, Markham's younger brother had left for Mexico. His brother had pleaded with him to go along, but Markham had refused. He doubted he would ever see him again. There could be no coming home for his brother now, not after abandoning the place where he was born and raised, not after turning his back on family.

With all the generations of family buried on the hacienda and the prosperity he had enjoyed, there was no way that Don Luis Markham would ever give it all up, no matter who asked. Whatever it took to keep what he had worked to build, he would do. Political men on either side of any particular border always proved to be the same—and it hadn't been that difficult to make the inroads. Keeping those inroads active was of utmost importance, and he would see to it that the right palms felt the strength of gold.

Another haul from the gambling tables in Los Angeles couldn't be counted on again for many years, if ever. Local law enforcement had already posted security in and around the gambling halls. But since the search centered on Joaquín Murrieta, he felt secure in believing that he could continue to raid gambling halls and faro and monte tables in the mining towns.

He had, in fact, been overseeing such raids for six months. The press believed Joaquín Murrieta, or members of gangs related to him, to be responsible. Why should anyone think different? As long as Joaquín Murrieta was on the loose, the door would be wide open for any number of raids that could be blamed on him.

His only concern now, and he hoped that it was unfounded, was that the *pistolero,* John Dimas, and the old man, Percival, were still alive. Dimas had killed or wounded many of his men already. Dimas knew what Percival had told him and what he had seen with his own eyes. It could prove to be a problem.

But he had gone to the place on the beach where his men had shot Dimas. He had seen the blood for himself, where Dimas had made his stand behind some rocks. Two of his Indian slaves, two Miwoks named Cholok and Ramón, seemed to believe that the *pistolero* had died. They said their information came from some of the slave women. They had discovered the old man, Percival, hauling Dimas's body away on a burro. Trenton Sterns, before leaving with the vaqueros and politicians, had said the same thing—that Elisa at the boardinghouse believed him to be dead.

"She should know," Sterns had said emphatically. "Likely her father told her, or maybe she even saw the body."

If the *pistolero* was gone, so much the better, but the old man had to be found and disposed of as well. Some day someone might take him seriously regarding what he knew and what he had seen. After all, no man who forged himself a high position went without enemies in equally high positions.

As for Sterns, Markham had no desire to keep him in his service any longer. Sterns knew better than to try and cause him trouble. He had his own life to live, and if he wanted to make it a good one, he would forget the past. His one last job, though, was very important.

The run to the north with the vaqueros and Sterns along to baby-sit the politicians would serve a double purpose: Yes, there was a lucrative market for horses in the camps all along the foothill country and, even more beneficial, it would serve as a front for acquiring more gold and valuables. Men that Markham had sent ahead to scout already knew the best places to rob.

As long as Joaquín Murrieta rode the trails and kept the citizens of California reading about his exploits in the newspapers, Don Luis Markham could continue to take advantage of it and grow more and more powerful.

After three days at the boardinghouse, Dimas had gained enough strength to make a move elsewhere. Elisa and Carlotta secured him in a produce wagon and smuggled him into an area where Joaquín and his gang often spent time while in the Los Angeles area.

"It's a beautiful place, and you'll like it," Carlotta told him. "The water falls down off stone that looks rough and bubbly, like pudding."

"Puddingstone," Elisa said with a laugh.

Dimas liked the area immediately. A multitude of springs and small streams came together among a series of wooded hills formed from volcanic rock. Within the hills lay a small basin where fresh water provided an abundance of lush grass and shoreline vegetation. Land birds and waterfowl alike made their homes in and around the water that found its way out of the basin and over a rocky falls, where it splashed into foam amidst more rock formations.

Above the falls rose a high, timbered hilltop that overlooked two separate valleys. It was easy to see why Joaquín Murrieta might pick a place like this to camp.

Elisa and Carlotta provided him with a large bag of cooked beef and cornmeal, along with selected wild fruits that grew in the area. Tasty and nutritious, it would keep for a very long time and provide what he needed for his healing and survival.

The cool morning air, crystal clear with every sunrise, kept him alert and his mind off his wounds. On occasion, the two women came to visit, bringing fresh tortillas and cooked stews and soups. They never stayed long, always anxious to get back to the children, whom they had left with trusted townsfolk. The one time Manuel came to visit with his mother, Elisa had a difficult time getting him to return with her.

He had with him a small piece of gray cloth, cut in the outline of a burro and stuffed with straw, with buttons sewn on for eyes and a piece of black cloth for the nose. Manuel and Francis had presented it to him.

"This is to remember my brother and me," he had said, blinking away a tear as he handed the burro to him. "Mother says that when your legs are good again, you're going away and will not return."

He thanked Manuel for the stuffed burro and said "Take good care of Carlotta and your mother. They are two very good people."

Life at Puddingstone was a combination of *Gulliver's Travels* and an occasional discussion with a passing shepherd or goat herder. Dimas felt vulnerable at times, his mobility strongly affected by his leg wounds, but the herders seemed to ignore that he might be at any disadvantage and suggested to him that the area was indeed a place of angels. Their interactions were always cordial, with Dimas and the herder wishing one another well and a good holiday season.

Christmas festivities brought extra light and laughter to Los Angeles and the small outlying districts. From his position at the top of the hill, Dimas could hear the faint sounds of the festivities in the distance. All seemed safe and secure. He wondered if the two padres hadn't chosen the holiday season to travel, believing the dangers to be greatly reduced.

After the New Year's festivities, the lights below grew faint and infrequent in comparison. For the most part, Dimas was alone with the quail and the jays and the night breezes. Occasionally, rain filled the valleys with drizzle and fog, then was gone when the songbirds ordered it. When the sun grew high, lizards skipped over the rocks to set themselves rigid and eye him. Elk and an occasional bear passed by, and the deer stared and then moved on while foraging for newly sprouted buds.

In his solitude, he discovered himself thinking a great deal about Maura Walsh. They had made some connection between them that he couldn't readily understand—a deep connection that made him feel he had always known her in some way. He couldn't explain it, and it had never happened to him before. He had met and nearly married a young woman some years before, which had ended when she decided to return to the east with her family. Since then, his excursions into romance had followed no particular pattern and had never gained any momentum.

He knew very little about Maura from the regular perspective, except he believed that he knew much more about her, and she about him, than either of them could have attained simply through their limited discussions. They had never had the time or the inclination to share anything on a deep level. Yet it seemed to him that he knew her well. The more he pondered it, the more mysterious it became.

He decided to let it go, for the chances of ever seeing her again were slim to none at best. Her decision to return to San Francisco and her former life and his quest to find Ricardo would certainly take them in separate directions. That's what he allowed himself to believe, though inside, somehow, he knew better.

They were two weeks past Tulare Lake, a huge body of water some fifty to sixty miles long and equally wide. While passing through the lower end of the camps, Maura had seen every kind of dress that could be found among the many different cultures represented. Most wore the everyday work clothes that suited their labor, which was elbow to elbow in the streams. Men and women alike toiled from before first light to well after dark, working together and often in teams, scratching through pans and rockers and sluices to separate the gold from the dirt and gravel.

The children frequently left the wagons to search among the miners for their parents. Maura spent considerable time coaxing them back, assuring them that if they would help her, she would make signs with their names on them and hang them on the wagons. One small girl was reunited with an uncle, who had to inform her that both her parents had succumbed to typhoid fever.

The presence of the priests allowed for safe travel and at times attracted men and women who wanted to be saved, or to have them extradite heathens from one camp or another. Father Francis told Maura that should a person care to explore, they could find all manner of individual represented in the diggings.

Agnes Sterns stayed within herself for the most part. She avoided any lengthy discussions with Maura, and though she tried to present herself as doing just fine, Maura could see that her breakup with Trenton had affected her deeply.

Maura sought a means by which to discuss it with Agnes, but the older woman avoided any circumstance that might afford that opportunity. Agnes had been forced by the priests to give up her wine and spent considerable time either sleeping or off by herself. There seemed to Maura to be a chasm developing between herself and the older woman, one not of her own choosing.

She wondered if Agnes could somehow read her mind, could see the images of John Dimas that appeared daily. She could recall his voice with ease and see his eyes with a special glow in them as he looked at her.

It perplexed her. She barely knew him, or at least it seemed that way. In another way, she thought she might have always known him and had actually been waiting to find him somewhere.

On a late afternoon, they entered San Andreas, a well-established mining town that rocked with revelry.

The sun had just set, and even in a steady rain, miners and saloon women and every form of onlooker filled the streets, drinking and dancing and laughing. Maura learned from Father Francis, who had been approached by one of the townspeople, that someone had discovered a large vein of ore nearby, filled with gold. It required celebration by everyone.

"Let's find a quieter district," Father Francis suggested, "where the activity is more subdued."

Toward the edge of town, they left the wagons and the children, well attended by a number of men and women who were eager just to rest for a while. Agnes declined to accompany them, but Maura followed the two priests into a community hall where festivities were the order of the evening. A band had set up on a plank stage in one corner, complete with fiddle, guitar, accordion, and marimbas.

"You will see something of interest, I believe," Father Francis told her. "Culturally speaking, of course."

Maura took note that the hall's inhabitants were primarily Hispanic people, with a few other ethnic groups as well. Dancers were getting ready to begin a fandango.

The women's gowns were cut with a European flavor, with short sleeves and, owing to the absence of corsets, a looser waist than the old style. The cloth was calicoes and silks, as well as crepes and cotton, set off by brightly colored sashes and belts, along with bold necklaces and earrings. Their footwear was satin or kid leather, and not one women could be seen with a bonnet. Their hair spilled down loose or in long braids.

"The fandango came over from Spain," Father Francis explained. "It had a certain context there, but the word 'fandango' has come to mean 'dance' in general here."

Maura followed in line and selected from a long table filled with huckleberries and roast mutton. A pail filled with mussels graced one end and a wide assortment of breads and tortillas covered yet another table.

Maura settled at a table with the priests, to dine and enjoy the entertainment.

"If you watch," Father Francis pointed out, "you will see a certain order to the fandango, as it was first introduced. That man, the *tecolero,* is the head, or the dancing master, if you will. He will introduce the women, seated over there, to the men, who are usually on horseback. Their spurs hang across their saddles, which means they are ready to dance. Here, tonight, they just hold their spurs up, which means the same thing."

The *tecolero* selected a lady and began the dance. The other men formed a line, and in a short time one of them cut in. Soon the area was covered with dancers, laughing and shouting and clapping to the music.

"If done the old way," Father Francis added, "it is all very formal and proper." He swallowed a bite of food. "We could have stopped at any number of places, but the dance here is given to the proper etiquette of civilized society. One can always find something different, if one looks for it, and desires such a thing."

Sterns rode with Bestez and the politicians down a narrow trail to where it broke into a bottom covered with tents and log cabins. Steep hillsides rose on both sides, where more structures seemed to teeter precariously, waiting for a clap of thunder to send them rolling downward.

A steady rain rendered the late afternoon dense and gloomy. The townsfolk, however, saw more reason for celebration than gloom in the weather. The muddy streets were clogged, and the noise rang up and down the gulch.

Bestez and the vaqueros erected their tents and the politicians took shelter with a bottle and active discussion about the upcoming evening. Bestez had promised them the best time of the entire trip.

"What's the name of this place?" Sterns asked.

"I believe this is called Troubled Gulch," Bestez replied. "It used to be called Trueblood Gulch, but I suppose the second name is more fitting, eh?" He laughed.

"How come it's not on the map?"

Bestez shrugged. "Who can say when it grew here, or how long it will remain. Such is the nature of these places." He laughed again. "The people might all be gone tomorrow. Word has come that another strike, new and bigger, was found not far from here, at San Andreas." Bestez licked his lips. "Must be some riches flowing, wouldn't you say?"

Sterns felt a strong knot form in his stomach. A select group of Markham's men had robbed numerous camps during the trip, well ahead of the horse herd. Now, just over half of the horses had been sold for gold or banknotes or traded for provisions Markham could use. Bestez would no doubt decide to take the good fortune from San Andreas as well and gain more favor from his boss.

The politicians knew nothing of these raids but believed instead that the gold ingots and other valuables that Bestez had bestowed upon them had been the result of well-honed gambling techniques and the desire of Don Luis Markham to share this good fortune. Despite the gifts, the trip had so far left them sore and irritable. There had been no time for engaging themselves in what they had been promised.

Their interests lay strictly in discovering for themselves the wild fandangos and back-alley liaisons they had heard so much about. Bestez had promised them their enjoyment, when the time was right.

With complete darkness, Sterns's anxieties deepened. Bestez and the vaqueros had planned their raid and now drew cards to see who would go along and who remain behind to watch the horses.

"It's time to take the politicians to their fun," Bestez told Sterns. "See that they enjoy themselves."

Sterns led the three into the middle of the gulch and tied his horse to a rail in front of a large tent saloon. The politicians, barely able to contain themselves, jumped from their saddles and handed Sterns the reins.

"Have some patience," Sterns told them. "We need to stay together here."

They paid him no mind and headed into the saloon. Smoke billowed out into the wet night from the open flaps. The rain muffled the noise within. Sterns quickly tied the horses and followed them inside.

The front area was laid out with log planks, to serve as bars for drinking or gambling. A second and much larger area opened behind.

The din rang in Sterns's ears. The politicians had

already secured a couple of bottles and had shouldered their way into the main tent to view the dancing.

Sterns found them and again asked them to stick together in a group. One of them pulled him in close and shouted in his face.

"I've been looking forward to this, don't you know." The others hooted and fell in with him. "So don't be acting like no schoolmarm."

"You are aware, gentlemen, that we need to get an early start tomorrow," he shouted back.

"Just roust me when it's time," another one of them said, "and send whatever lady I happen to be with back home."

They laughed again and passed the bottles between them. Sterns turned to the dancing, a raucous mix of Spanish flamenco from an old and battered guitar of a burly Mexican miner and off-key accompaniment by two Yankee fiddlers. The dancers, mostly Yankee miners and a mix of women, Hispanic being dominant, clung to each other, pawing and removing clothing as they laughed and drank and churned their way around the dance area.

Sterns shielded himself from dripping rainwater as best he could. The roof was nothing but tattered remnants of other tents and wagon tops and lengths of various cloths—anything that could be sewn or tied or otherwise patched together in some fashion—all held up by tree trunks hewn of their branches and planted in rows on two sides, leaving the middle open.

It was hideous to behold and would never serve as an adequate roof anywhere else, but it gave some protection from the downpour. It leaked badly, and the dancers' feet splattered mud in liquid brown sheets. Lanterns bounced as the dancers slid into the posts they hung from. It had become an almost nightly tradition. No matter the weather, the fandango in the center of camp could be counted on.

Sterns felt a hand on his shoulder. He was roughly turned around. Bestez leaned forward.

"There's been a change of plans."

"I'll get the politicians," Sterns said quickly.

"I didn't say that," Bestez yelled. "You watch them closely, Señor Sterns. Do you understand?"

"Where are you going?"

"The horse herd is gone. Some of the men are dead. I have to take the others and make the raiders pay."

"What are you talking about?"

"What's the matter with your ears? I said someone raided us."

"Why don't I get the politicians and we'll all go back to camp together?"

"No, let them have their fun. Tell them to gamble and have their women and that Don Luis Markham is happy to entertain them."

"I don't know."

"Do it! I will get the horses back and I will make the *bandidos* pay for their indiscretion. Then tomorrow we will take the politicians and their sick stomachs the rest of the way up to Sacramento."

TWELVE

Maura left the fandango with the priests and returned to camp. Most of the children were fast asleep. A few remained awake, waiting for her to return.

As she arrived, one of the women watching them smiled at her. "They say they want you for a mother now."

Maura had already been thinking about establishing retreats of some kind for orphaned children in the camps. When she returned to San Francisco, she would set up a business fund for just such an endeavor. If she could somehow find the right people, of the same quality and commitment as Elisa in Los Angeles, she could construct a chain of homes in the main mining towns. Children who had lost their parents in one way or another would at least have a safe place to live.

"Tell them," Maura said to the woman, "that they will be cared for by someone, and not to worry."

"But it is you they want."

The pressing needs of the growing number of orphaned children had created new drive in Maura. She had managed to put Trenton Sterns behind her and focus on what she wanted for herself and how she might best be able to accomplish it. A lot of work needed to be done to develop a sound plan to bring growing numbers of orphaned children to a place of safety.

The camps grew more dangerous with each passing day. Ore wasn't being mined in the quantities it had been even a year earlier. Still, ever more gold seekers made their way over the Sierras or docked in San Francisco, Monterey, or Los Angeles every week, and ever more children were eventually left alone due to circumstances they didn't understand. The streams had become a tight squeeze for little or no gain. The pressures caused those with the strongest gambling urges to migrate from gulch to gulch on a mere whim, often forgetting where they had been the previous day, occasionally forgetting, in some cases, where they had left their children.

The more she traveled through the gold camps, the more Maura believed any circumstance could present itself. They had already picked up a half-dozen children during their journey. In Angel's Camp, Maura discovered a small boy and his sister rummaging through garbage.

"Ma died of coughing when we first got here," the small boy explained. "We moved here, and a week past, Pa said he was going to get his gold back and that we was to sit tight. That was a week past. It's just me and Janie now."

Two more children added to the number that needed a secure place to recover from their loss. With the way the system worked, discovering these children at unusual times in unusual places, Maura realized that a commitment to Trenton Sterns could never have worked out anyway. He would have expected certain things from her at certain times, especially from a social standpoint, and conflict would have been the order of every day. She would have felt she needed to be at the orphanage when he would have insisted she attend an event sponsored by Markham. She couldn't have been wife to a politician in any sense of the word.

Despite their differences, Maura hoped Trenton Sterns might have a good life. As she readied herself for bed, Agnes Sterns appeared, her eyes wet with tears.

"I haven't had the wherewithal to talk to you, Maura," she began. "Please forgive me."

"There's nothing to forgive," Maura told her.

"Maybe I can't have you as a daughter-in-law," Agnes continued, "but I don't want to lose you as a friend."

Maura hugged her. Agnes allowed more tears to flow.

"You'll still keep the same place in my heart," Agnes added. "I want you to visit me as often as you can."

"Perhaps there is no reason to have to say goodbye at all," Maura suggested. "Why don't you assist me with my plans for the orphanages? You could coordinate the efforts from San Francisco."

Agnes was quick to answer. "I believe I would like that. I could be of good help to you. I will still have to keep an eye on Trenton, though. He will always need that."

"You can have as much time as you need," Maura told her. "I know how much you think of Trent and I'm sorry things turned out the way they did, but everything works out for the best."

"That's the way I've always seen it," Agnes agreed. "As hard as it is to take at times, you just have to believe that's true."

Sterns felt himself engulfed by the crowd. The noise grew louder, the dancing wilder. The politicians had lost themselves within the churning mass of people.

Each one had found a female partner whose hands moved quickly and deliberately.

Sterns noticed one of them in the corner with a scantily clad woman. He filled her hands with gold ingots. She laughed and grabbed a hat from a nearby dancer and dropped the gold into it.

A group of men appeared at the back and began to watch the dancers closely. Sterns took no particular note that their faces were blackened with a mixture of soot and dark soil.

He did notice the scantily clad dancer haul the politician into the center of the room, where everyone moved back while she began to undress him. He seemed not to mind, but went along with it playfully.

She exposed his middle, and three women from the crowd appeared beside her. They retreated, and the dancer ran a long knife into the politician's midsection. He stared at her. After three more hard thrusts, his knees buckled and he fell forward into the mud. Rain leaked through the roof onto his back.

Sterns stood rooted in shock. The music stopped and amid some screaming and yelling, the crowd retreated. The men with blackened faces shot their pistols into the air and pressed forward. They began robbing saloon patrons at gunpoint while some of them herded the remaining politicians into the center of the room.

Sterns rushed toward them, and a large man with a grizzled beard and a dusty red sombrero cut him off. His blackened face shone with sweat.

"Let them have their fun," he told Sterns.

He felt the man's firm grip on his arm. The thumb and forefinger were missing from his right hand.

Sterns struggled against him. "I can't allow this to happen."

"You must allow it, Señor," the big man insisted. "They must pay for their crimes."

The big man held Sterns back while the men and three women with them knifed and shot the other two politicians.

"This can't be happening," Sterns said.

"Yes, it can be happening," the big man said. "Those men take from the people, you know that. They never give back, so we're giving them something to remember."

"Who are you, and how did you know who those men are?"

"Let's just say there are those who are watching Don Luis Markham closely," he replied.

Sterns felt a pistol barrel against his back. The gun exploded and he fell forward into the mud. The big man with the red sombrero, missing the thumb and forefinger on his right hand, leaned over Sterns and emptied his pistol into his body. He stepped back and smiled while his men grabbed Sterns and the politicians by their feet and dragged them out the back, into the rain and darkness.

Maura and Agnes Sterns helped a group of women wash breakfast dishes. The rain had vanished and the skies were clear. A bright sun rose over the hills, bathing new flowers and blossoms in golden light.

As they worked, Agnes commented again and again on what Maura had told her about the previous evening and the interesting festivities.

"I wish now that I had attended," she commented. "I hadn't realized theirs was such a vibrant culture."

"That fandango was amazing to watch," Maura told her.

"It's good that they can keep their sense of values with all the changes," Agnes said. "It can't be easy for them."

"Change is born of conflict," Agnes stated. "It's always been that way."

A group of miners rode into camp and dismounted. Father Francis and Father Manuel greeted them.

"We're in need of a priest over at Troubled Gulch," one of them stated. "For last rites."

"What happened?" Father Francis asked.

"Joaquín Murrieta struck. He robbed a saloon and killed four men."

The padres made the sign of the cross. "Does anyone know these men who were killed?" Father Francis asked.

Another one of the men replied, "Word has it they were politicians from Sacramento, looking for a good time."

Maura and Agnes stiffened.

"They got a lot more than they figured on, and there was no way to stop it," the man finished.

Father Francis told the men to wait a moment and walked over to Maura and Agnes.

"I fear the worst," he said. "God willing, not so. But who else could it be?"

"You stay here, Agnes," Maura said. "I'll go with Father Francis and Father Manuel."

Agnes had already covered her face with trembling hands. "Oh, no. It can't be so."

"I'll learn what happened and tell you," Maura promised her.

"Are you certain you want to do this?" Father Francis asked.

"Yes," Maura replied. "I have to."

Troubled Gulch had grown much calmer. A group of miners had formed a posse and were in the hills, after the bandits. Those who had stayed behind did not celebrate but stood talking about the previous night and staring at the bodies lying in front of the tent saloon. A storekeeper had covered them with a tarp, but their feet stuck out the bottom.

Maura arrived with the two priests and a few of the men from the caravan. Her interest did not lie in viewing Trenton Sterns's body, but in gaining an understanding of why he had died.

"Those bandits had it in for those men, that was plain," she overheard an onlooker say. He owned the tent saloon. "The way they were dressed, they didn't belong out here."

Another man came forward, an older miner, and spoke directly to the saloonkeeper. "They had it coming. Lawmakers is lawbreakers. That's the way I see it."

"Is there any other type of individual out here?" the saloonkeeper asked. "I'll admit to shorting drinks when the drinker can't count change."

"That's not the same as shorting a whole state of citizen folk," the old miner insisted.

Maura approached him. "Did you know any of the deceased, sir?"

"Can't say that I did, no."

"Then how are you able to judge them?"

"Begging your pardon, ma'am," the miner said, "but I've come across this whole damned country, trapping furs and now to the diggings, here. All the damned way, by God! It was all fair until the civilized part of things showed up. All good until then."

"I'll ask you again, sir, did you know any of these men personally?"

"I just told you no."

"And I'm telling you again that just because you don't agree with the way things are, you can't condemn another for the part you believe he played in it."

The old miner frowned.

"Would you have done this to these men?"

"I ain't no bandit," he said quickly.

"Does the word bandit mean killer?" she asked.

The saloonkeeper interceded. "She has a point. Nobody should die like this."

The old miner turned and walked away. Everyone gathered around the bodies, and the tarps were removed. Each priest made the sign of the cross over himself and began to pray.

Maura's knees buckled, and she slumped to the street. Two men helped her to her feet.

"You hadn't ought to see this, ma'am," one of them said.

"Why should anyone have to?" she asked.

All four men were covered, head to foot, in mud and dried blood. The raiders had dragged them through the streets behind their horses before leaving them in crumpled heaps in front of the saloon.

"Why would Joaquín Murrieta do this?" Maura added.

"He has a hate that runs deep," the saloonkeeper replied. "If someone doesn't stop him, there'll be more and more of this kind of thing. Just more and more."

When the priests finished with the last rites, they met with Maura to discuss burial plans.

"We should inter them here," Father Francis said. "It's not practical to think we can take them on with us."

Maura agreed. "It's just that Agnes Sterns never in her wildest dreams thought her son's final resting place would be a lonely mining camp in a forgotten gulch of the Sierra Nevada foothills."

Markham sat his horse on a hill overlooking the ocean. The afternoon had come and gone without any sign of Bestez and the vaqueros. They should have arrived a number of afternoons before this. Bestez had better have a very good excuse.

During their absence there had been no disturbances of any kind. No one had tried to steal horses or to make trouble in any way. Perhaps everyone was right: Joaquín Murrieta would never return to Los Angeles.

Markham already knew that Sterns and the politicians had been killed. The papers had reported the deaths of "some men of upper class," as yet unidentified. It wouldn't be long before their names came out. That would complicate things even more. Personal friends at the upper levels of state government aren't killed by *bandidos* without repercussions. No doubt Joaquín Murrieta would have to pay, and pay dearly.

Markham noted a line of dust rising skyward in the distance. The dust grew and materialized into Bestez and some of the vaqueros who had gone with him. But not all of them. In fact, less than half.

When his foreman rode up to greet him, he said, "I want to know everything. You understand? Leave nothing out."

"We encountered a lot of misfortune," Bestez responded "We have a lot of gold, but lost horses and men to Joaquín."

"Yes, I believe Joaquín stole the horses. But who killed Sterns and the politicians?"

"His cousin, Three-Fingered Jack. But the papers will say it was Joaquín."

"Ah! I don't want to hear that!" Markham spat the

words. "If Joaquín is found and stopped, how can we go on with our plans?"

"That is true," Bestez agreed. "I wonder what will happen, though. The people are screaming for justice. How badly will those in Sacramento want Joaquín now?"

For Dimas, his continued life at Puddingstone, in full view of the Angeles Mountains, fell into a routine. He had become a part of his environment, living through each day separate from the one before, discounting the one to follow. Time as such held no measure, except for the course of the sun.

He read *Gulliver's Travels* twice and set it aside. His own journey had fallen into a place where he could do nothing to stop what flowed out of him. He came to realize the anxiety he faced in locating his brother had little to do with anything but their own relationship.

While his legs healed, he viewed his brother's face constantly. He tried to recall and understand the vivid differences that had come to tear them so far apart.

He had learned the solitary life well as a child while scouting the woods along the Missouri River, held fast in waking dreams of riding warrior ponies across the rugged mountains with his father. He often asked

Ricardo to accompany him, but his brother had no interest in emulating their father in any way, except for possibly gaining the upper hand over an enemy in hand-to-hand combat. Ricardo's days were spent with youths who shared his particular brand of rage, rousting their way through St. Louis's alleys, leaving a trail of blood and broken bones.

On one occasion, Ricardo accompanied him, just once. They had stumbled upon an old cabin up from the river's edge. During their snooping, they discovered an old table and several large, square nails made of iron. Ricardo had held them in his hands, fascinated, and had ventured a guess at their origin.

"Do you suppose these come from clear back in the Roman times?" he asked. "Like the same kind of nails they used on Jesús?"

Dimas had never forgotten the question, heartfelt, from some deep place within his brother.

When Dimas replied that Jesús was never in Missouri, Ricardo had responded quickly. "Mother says Jesús is everywhere, and that we must feel his pain to truly know eternal life."

"You don't need nails in your hands to feel pain," Dimas told his brother.

At that point, Ricardo drove a nail partway into his right hand, severing a nerve. His fingers twitched spasmodically.

"What did you do that for?" Dimas asked him.

Ricardo never answered but ran away instead. He never came back into the woods along the river. After that, the two of them began going their separate ways and eventually, as adults, lost contact completely. The letters from Stockton had been the first he had heard of Ricardo's whereabouts in a number of years.

Dimas had never regretted going his own way and following his own path. The lessons he had learned along the Missouri had served him well, both during and after the fighting in Texas and as a Ranger. Though Rangers usually traveled in pairs or small groups, more than once he had been forced to finish a detail alone when a partner had been shot and killed.

The search for his father had taken him several places, and each place he found himself, including his time as a Texas Ranger, took on a special meaning. This change, this promise to his dying mother and the turn toward seeking Ricardo, had an entirely different feel to it, and it troubled him deeply.

He had pondered over how he would approach Joaquín Murrieta and what he would say. "Let me talk to you about one of your men. I'm looking for my no-good brother." Or perhaps, "My dead mother wants her youngest son to give up being a *bandido*. Hand him over to me."

He had never faced so daunting a task in his entire

life. He had chased any number and brand of thief and killer, and had fought in battles where it seemed he had lost all sense of sanity, but now he had to locate his brother and do all within his power to convince him to leave Joaquín Murrieta.

In the end, to what avail, though? And was it even possible? Ricardo had turned from the family, had left, and had not seen his mother in years. There seemed little doubt that he had no clue of her death.

The letters had indicated that he wanted to become someone remembered by all. Not for the sake of conforming to everyone else, but just the opposite. He wanted to elevate himself to the status of a leader. How was that in keeping with the nail he had pierced his hand with as a child? Perhaps he had already found a means by which to martyr himself.

Yes, perhaps Percival was right: Ricardo might already be dead—hanged or shot or knifed, left along a road or trail for the scavengers or, at best, buried in a shallow and forgotten grave. What good would it do to risk himself in a losing effort to find a brother who had always hated him? How could that possibly serve his poor mother's wishes?

He couldn't escape the discussion with Father Francis. Nor could he erase the look on his mother's face when he had promised he would "bring Ricardo back from the edge of hell." The statement, as soon as he had uttered it, had taken on a haunting quality. He had in effect promised to endure anything to see to it that his brother left Joaquín Murrieta.

THIRTEEN

Dimas tossed and turned in his sleep. Try as he might to pull in the reins, his horse carried him ever onward, in a floating motion, toward a distant and secret place. A place he didn't want to go.

When he arrived, he found himself standing on a hillside, the horse nowhere to be seen.

Riders in the distance motioned to him. One of them yelled in Spanish, "Over here. You're supposed to be with us."

The hideout stood in the lower end of a canyon, of no notable interest, just a collection of old adobe buildings where the odor of horses hung strongly in the air. Mustangs paced within cordons of rope, secured by watching *mesteneros,* vaqueros whose purpose in life had come to focus on rounding up wild horses.

They seemed to float easily as they rode toward him. Their faces were heavily blackened with soil and soot, and their hands, as they held the reins of their horses, dripped thin drops of blood onto saddles lined with wisps of human hair.

"Ricardo?" Dimas asked one of them. "Where is Ricardo?"

The vaqeuro pointed to an opening in a grove of trees, near a small creek, where a group of men were gathered, all pointing and shouting. They presented an odd mix: Yankees, as well as Chinese, Miwok and Chumash Indian miners, and an assortment of businesspeople of all ethnic groups. All had gathered for some event.

Dimas felt himself moving, floating, to the edge of the assembly. They nodded and watched him take a position off to one side to view the proceedings. He couldn't move from the spot, but was held fast, by some unseen weight, as the scene unfolded before him.

He watched while a young man of obvious power, dressed in bearskin chaps and a brightly colored cotton shirt, pointed horsehide boots, the rowels on his spurs large and of pure silver, addressed the gathering. The young man's sash held two large revolvers and a Bowie knife sheathed in bearskin. His hair flowed to the base of his neck, red-gold and curly, from under his dusty sombrero, which itself appeared lit with a kind of white-gold light.

Dimas knew he had seen this man before. He struggled to remember where. It had been in a place of judgment, the room where they had condemned Joaquín Murrieta for the death of General Joshua Bean. The red-blond man at the door, who had disappeared during the testimony.

Dimas turned. One of the riders sat his horse beside him, his face lit with a broad smile.

"Yes, you know him. We call him El Famoso."

The young man was definitely in charge. His face held a look of indifference as he took a large basin of water from one of his assistants and began to wash his hands. He motioned to a man on his knees in front of him, his wrists bound tightly behind his back. He finished washing his hands and took a towel from the assistant.

The man on his knees turned toward Dimas. His face was covered with blood from a crown of acacia thorns that had been driven into his skull.

"John, can you save me?"

"Ricardo!"

"It's too late," said the man with the red-gold hair. "Everyone has spoken."

"You can stop this!" Dimas argued. "You have the power!"

"My hands are clean of it. Can't you see that?"

Two of the attendees jerked Ricardo to his feet and untied his wrists. They strung a rope around his neck and secured the loose end to section of oak sapling, cut from a larger trunk and hewn of its branches. Dimas watched while they fitted a much smaller branch through the rope around his brother's neck and had him grasp both ends with his hands. He could either save himself from choking or not, while dragging the section of tree trunk behind him.

El Famoso pointed at Dimas. "You are going along with him." He motioned to his men. "Take him!"

Dimas was forced to follow behind his brother, who received lashes from members of the gathering as he struggled toward the top of a nearby hill. Their horsewhips loomed large above their heads as they sent blow after blow against Ricardo's bare back. At the top of the hill, three heavy oak tree trunks had been planted in a row.

Ricardo collapsed. Dimas noticed another man standing nearby. Trenton Sterns, held fast by two vaqueros. His eyes appeared vacant and lifeless.

"What are you doing here?" Dimas asked.

Sterns didn't answer but submitted without protest as they threw him to his back.

"Did you hear me?" Dimas pressed.

Sterns looked up. "What's the matter with you? Can't you see that I'm dead?"

They tied him with short lengths of rope to a cross member made of an oak sapling. Two horsemen then hauled the sapling into place while two other men tied it securely to one of the heavy posts buried upright in the ground.

Dimas could offer no resistance as they forced him down and tied him to a sapling, then hauled him up and fastened him in the same manner they had Sterns. The gathering of people, men and women alike, watched in solemn silence. El Famoso, his eyes fixed on Ricardo, wept openly.

Dimas turned to his brother. They had fastened him to the cross with the old nails from the cabin beside the river. They were much larger than he had remembered them those many years ago, and stained red. Ricardo's hands and fingers jerked spasmodically.

"Ricardo?" Dimas yelled. "Get us out of this."

Ricardo smiled. "Where's your faith, big brother?"

"My faith?"

"You knew what you are getting into."

"I had to do it. You know that."

"I have to do this, and take you with me."

Someone from the crowd advanced to the foot of Ricardo's cross. He held a Californio's long lance. Dimas turned away as it was thrust into Ricardo's side.

The skies darkened and Ricardo bowed his head. Dimas began to yell for him to come back, but his brother had expired.

Still Dimas continued to yell. He struggled to break

free, but his bonds held him tight, and his feeling of being trapped only increased with each passing moment. It increased still more when he noticed his pistol fall to the ground at the base of the cross.

"No!" he yelled.

"You there!" one of the men below shouted. "Quiet yourself!"

Dimas spit at him. The man motioned to one of the others and pointed to where another oaken cross member lay on the ground. After receiving the cross member, the man looked up at Dimas.

"This should take care of it," he said flatly.

With all his might, the man drove the cross member into Dima's right leg, just above the knee. Dimas choked with pain. He hadn't yet caught his breath before the left leg bore a crushing second blow.

Dimas felt himself sagging. He looked down. His body pushed past his knees, the broken splinters of bone protruding from his legs. He felt himself dropping deeper and deeper, farther and farther, toward a place he had never been before.

Dimas jerked awake and looked at his legs. Neither was broken, nor was he hanging from a cross with his brother beside him.

Elisa and Carlotta shook him vigorously.

"Señor Dimas," Elisa said, "you sleep like the dead."

"Dreams of the dead, perhaps," Carlotta ventured.

"Perhaps," Dimas acknowledged. He sat up. Thunder rolled overhead. "I guess I lost track of time."

"It's Good Friday," Elisa said. "We wanted you to have something special for Easter."

He saw that they had both brought skin bags, Elisa's being particularly large.

"You look strong, for a hermit," she said.

"Scraggly, but strong," Carlotta added. She produced a straight razor. "You will need to boil some water and clean yourself up. A padre must be presentable to everyone."

Elisa opened the large bag and removed a brown robe.

"Try it on," she told Dimas.

Dimas had finally awakened fully. "I don't say that many rosaries any more," he told her.

"You need to start, and to learn how to say mass as well," she insisted.

"What?" Dimas protested.

"He's right," Carlotta agreed. "Saying mass would be a sacrilege. He should just stick to the other six days of the week."

"I don't even know what you two are talking about," Dimas said.

"How does the title, Father Dimas, sound to you?" Elisa ventured.

"Always one for jokes. But to lug that robe way up here?"

"I won't be taking it back with me."

"Hurry, see if it fits you," Carlotta insisted. She grabbed Dimas by the arm and pulled.

"How else are you going to keep from being killed by *bandidos?*" Elisa said.

"Did your father come to see you and suggest this?"

"Let's just say that he wants it this way, and not for you to ask questions about it. You can find him at San Gabriel."

"You're saying that it's time?"

"Finally," Elisa replied.

"But it seems you're not so anxious now," Carlotta observed. "What happened?"

"Maybe he sees a mirror with his brother's face in it," Elisa ventured.

"I'm not like my brother," Dimas protested. He leaned toward Elisa. "Your father even said the chances are good he's dead."

"The trip is shorter the sooner you leave," Elisa insisted.

"You two are tired of seeing me alive," Dimas said flatly.

"You've come through death already a number of times, Señor Dimas," Carlotta pointed out. "Your cat still has seven lives."

"Go to San Gabriel and begin it," Elisa said.

"Yes," Carlotta stated firmly. "Go and find Ricardo and tell him I miss him so much every day."

Dimas stared at her. "How do you know Ricardo?"

"He asked me to marry him."

"What?"

"The week before General Joshua Bean was killed, Joaquín and some of his men were visiting friends in Los Angeles. He came to be with me for a while. We came up to this very place."

"Too bad he's not here now," Dimas said.

"That would be too good and too easy," Carlotta agreed. "He insisted on going with Joaquín. You see, he sees Joaquín as someone to look up to and be like."

"He's always wanted to be famous for a cause," Dimas told her.

Carlotta blinked back tears. "We met a year ago, right here, when I was bringing supplies to the gang with some other women. They were going to Mexico with horses to sell. Then all this with the general happened. They all had to flee when it was said that Joaquín killed this man. I haven't seen Ricardo since."

"Maybe he'll come back here to see you," Dimas suggested.

"That will not happen, not for some time, if ever," she argued. "It's much too dangerous here for any of them."

"Something bad has started because of this General Bean thing," Elisa put in. "It will make Joaquín a hunted man. And if I know him, he will be glad for it. He will want it. He will cherish it."

"So, you can see that you must ride hard day and night to find Joaquín and his men," Carlotta insisted. "You must face your fears and find Ricardo. Not just for yourself, Señor Dimas, but for everyone around you as well."

With a horse Carlotta brought the following day and a supply of food and staples Elisa heaped upon him, Dimas set out toward the southern mines. He knew only that he wanted to reach the area south of the Mokelumne River, where the Calaveras, Stanislaus, Tuolumne, and Merced rivers flowed through the Sierra Nevada foothill country. He could only guess at which of the many camps he might start his search.

Elisa and Carlotta had told him that Sonora and Angel's Camp were principal hangouts for Joaquín and his men. "He likes to play and deal monte, his favorite card game," Elisa had informed him. "Ask where a monte game is going on and you could find him there."

Dimas wondered if he might ever get used to the robe, together with the large wooden rosary and crucifix that he had tied around his waist. The robe itself felt scratchy but of more concern was the large bullet hole left in the lower right side of the fabric, its circular pattern stained a dark brown around and below it.

"Who would shoot a priest?" Dimas had asked the women.

"You may learn the answer to that yourself," Elisa replied.

"Just be certain," Carlotta added, "that you regard it as, 'Who would shoot *at* a priest?' "

Dimas put his finger in the hole. "Whoever fired the weapon didn't miss. Maybe this tunic is marked somehow."

"Death cannot find a padre's robe more than once," Carlotta responded. "I believe that's an old saying. Besides, it's the only one we could find."

"Surely the Church could spare a better one," Dimas protested.

"What would the Church say about you wearing even that one, let alone a new one?" Elisa asked. "So don't push for something better."

"I never asked for this one," Dimas replied. "The both of you turn this around."

"If you're going to find Joaquín and your brother,

Ricardo," Carlotta stated, "it's time for you to meet with Percival and learn what you must from him."

Dimas rode toward San Gabriel Mission in the late afternoon. A heavy fog had settled in the night before and hadn't lifted. A few miles from the mission, a small man riding Percival's burro emerged from the misty evening.

"Please, do not be alarmed," the small man said in Spanish. "Percival himself asked that I speak with you."

The instructions were precise.

"At nightfall, you are to go to the far end of an underground tunnel that runs from below the mission, and then go up into the cover of trees and brush. Percival will meet you there."

"Near a tunnel?"

"You know Percival to be an unusual person," the small man persisted. He got down from the burro and handed the halter to Dimas. "Please, just do as he wishes and leave him to the shadows."

After sleeping a few hours, Dimas awakened in the dark. His wounds still ached with stiffness in the damp air, but he had learned that frustration and quick movement did not hold the answer. The fog had grown denser, and the night promised a miserable time for him.

Leading the burro, he rode his horse into the trees and brush where the tunnel emerged. It was well hidden, as the small man had suggested. There sat Percival, cross-legged, a blanket wrapped tightly around him.

"Just tie that pesky burro over there," he instructed Dimas.

Dimas followed instructions and started toward Percival.

"Not too close," he advised Dimas. "Let's just say it would bring bad luck."

"How's my luck been so far?" Dimas asked.

"Are you still breathing life?" He chuckled. "I'm glad. Fine night I picked for a meeting, wouldn't you say?"

"One night's as good as the next for me," Dimas replied.

"Do you want cheese with your whine? You sound like you've lost hope already."

"This is an odd way to meet," Dimas stated.

Percival adjusted his position slightly. "You'll have to take my word that I can't explain this circumstance to you. Perhaps at another time. Right now it would only serve to confuse you."

"Are you dead—a ghost or something?" Dimas asked.

Percival laughed. "Have you ever seen a ghost?"

"No, not before now."

"Then you have nothing to compare me to," Percival pointed out.

"Ghost or not, I find it odd."

"You're entitled to. Just listen carefully. That's the point here."

Dimas resolved to go along with whatever the old man's wishes might be and however he might approach finding Joaquín and his men. Percival explained that serious trouble had already occurred in some of the camps, the worst at a small tent town called Troubled Gulch, near San Andreas.

"Markham's politicians were killed," Percival explained. "Trenton Sterns as well."

"How did that happen?"

"They attended the wrong fandango. The papers are filled with all kinds of stories about Joaquín Murrieta. It wasn't him, but it's now very important for you to find your brother as soon as you can."

"The trails up there aren't hard to follow, I trust."

"Joaquín's not on the main trails. You'll need guides."

Dimas shifted and said, "It's getting more complicated."

"Do you know the Vereda del Monte?"

"Only by name. The main trail along the foothills to Mexico."

"Knowing it by name only won't help you. You'll go to Markham's ranch," Percival instructed. "There you will find two Miwok Indians who will scout for you. His two main slaves. I know them and have ridden with them and their father."

"Should I bring Markham a bottle of wine, in case he doesn't remember me?"

Percival laughed. "He thinks you're dead."

"My face will tell him otherwise."

"Just do what I tell you," Percival insisted. "I've watched Markham around priests, and he never gets too close to them. He's more superstitious than me, even. He believes that if a man of the cloth sees the look of the devil in a man's eyes, he'll be forever damned."

"Do the Miwoks know Joaquín?"

"No one knows Joaquín. But they do know where to find him."

"And then what?"

"Just do what you can to gain a little trust and that's all."

"After what's happened, I find it hard to believe Joaquín would trust even a Franciscan," Dimas pointed out.

"Certainly not a Franciscan *pistolero,*" Percival agreed.

"The robe becomes you. But your revolver pokes at the cloth, even in the darkness."

"I know more about the revolver than the rosary."

"Not any longer, not if you intend to fool Joaquín Murrietta." He marked Dimas's silence and continued. "I'm here to say that you can no longer be a *pistolero*. As good as you are, you will have to lay them aside."

Dimas recalled the dream, his pistol falling to the ground from where he hung next to Ricardo.

"If all you want to do is talk to your brother," he continued, "it shouldn't be a problem."

"I want to take him out of there, away from Joaquín's band."

"I'm certain he will listen to you."

"I promised my mother. To deliver him from hell."

"And you are the one to do that?" Percival shook a finger at him. "You can't make a promise that's not up to you."

"I must do what I can. I must succeed."

Percival waved him away. "You might be dressed like those who represent God, but you are not Him. When you go to Markham's, keep yourself lost in the fog."

FOURTEEN

Dimas arrived at Markham's headquarters as first light tried to pierce the fog. The haze lay thick and swirled with a light breeze. From somewhere on the property a confused rooster crowed.

As expected, Markham had yet to rise from his bed. His vaqueros were already busy with their work. Two servants eyed him from the ranch house and, as also expected, Bestez appeared in the doorway.

"I cannot see too well," he yelled out in Spanish.

"Don't you know a Franciscan when one appears?" Dimas yelled back. He felt confident that Bestez would never recognize him by voice, as his had been hoarse and nearly inaudible the last time they had met.

Bestez limped from the house. The knee injury had healed badly.

"A moment," Bestez yelled. He disappeared around

the house into the fog, yelled, and reappeared with two vaqueros.

The three men approached. Dimas fitted his hood tightly over his head, pulling the front down so that most of his face was in shadow.

They approached and all three made the sign of the cross. Dimas bowed slightly.

Bestez remained a distance from Dimas's horse. He didn't want to appear irreverent.

"Are you lost, Padre?" he asked.

Dimas responded, "Not if this ranch is owned by Don Luis Markham."

Bestez smiled. "Did you come here to save him?"

"I came to save some of you. Others, perhaps not."

Bestez grunted, as did the other two men.

"A cold and dismal day for a padre to be out," he said. "The Lord must have sent you for some reason that is difficult to see."

"If you are a pious man," Dimas told him, "you will kiss the crucifix." He held out the rosary that girdled his waist.

"I have kissed a great many of those," Bestez said, "but my plight is always the same."

"Try one more time," Dimas suggested. "Kiss it with your heart, not just your mouth."

Bestez never moved. Dimas offered the crucifix to

the other two men. One of them removed his sombrero and stepped forward, his face tightly grimaced. He slowly bent over and touched his lips to the crucifix, his eyes closed. He then stared into the dark recess under the cloak. Dimas's face was completely in shadow. He quickly stepped back.

Bestez asked in English, "What brings a man of the cloth to Don Luis Markham's ranch?"

Dimas leaned forward in the saddle and shrugged.

Bestez repeated the question in Spanish.

"I was told that there were some Indian men here who deserved to be free, who wanted to become scouts for someone like me," Dimas replied. "I would like to speak with them."

The three men frowned. Bestez said, "We don't know of any Miwoks."

"I didn't say they were Miwoks," Dimas pointed out. "Perhaps you don't care to be saved."

"If we give any of our men to you, without the permission of Don Luis," one of the others said, "you might grant us dispensation, but Don Luis would put us in hell."

"And where is Don Luis?" Dimas asked. "Maybe he would be so bold as to rebuke the Church also."

"Perhaps there is no need to bother Don Luis," Bestez suggested. "We will take you to where they live."

At the slaves' quarters, Bestez ordered all the Indian

men outside. They lined up in a formation familiar to all of them, nearly naked in the cold.

"Allow them blankets!" Dimas yelled.

Bestez spoke to the slaves and they hurried inside and returned into formation, each with a blanket wrapped around him.

"Will Cholok and Ramón please step forward," Dimas ordered.

"Wait," Bestez broke in. "You don't want them."

"They are the two I do want, Señor," Dimas corrected him. "By order of the Church."

"This I do not understand," Bestez protested. "What does the Church want with two Miwoks?"

"They are to assist me in the Lord's work," Dimas replied. "Would you contest that?"

Bestez turned to one of the vaqueros. "Don Luis might be awake by now."

"I asked you, Señor," Dimas pressed, "would you go against the Church?"

"I will leave that up to Don Luis," Bestez replied.

"Something he would do?" Dimas asked.

"Please, Padre. What is your name?" Bestez made the sign of the cross over himself.

Dimas didn't answer. He turned his attention back to the Indian men.

"Which of you is Cholok and which Ramón? You two are ordered to be my guides."

Cholok, slim but strongly built, spoke up in behalf of himself and Ramón, insisting that they were both excellent guides.

Dimas pointed. "Get what clothes you have and select a horse from Don Luis Markham's best horses, in that corral."

Bestez looked toward the main house. "Where is Don Luis?" he said under his breath.

"This is a good thing for you," Dimas told Bestez. "How did you get the limp?"

"An accident," Bestez replied.

"Perhaps, for doing this, you will be cured in time," Dimas suggested.

"Perhaps," Bestez acknowledged.

When the two Miwok men had gathered their things and were mounted, Dimas led them toward the main house. Bestez and the two vaqueros followed.

Upon seeing Markham on his veranda, Bestez rode hurriedly ahead. He and Markham talked and then Markham ventured only so far toward Dimas and stood with his hands on his hips.

Dimas raised the large wooden rosary around his waist. "You must kiss the feet of our Lord."

Markham remained at a distance. His head was bare, his hair tousled above his irate features.

"This is highly unusual," Markham said.

"Father Francis has instructed me, by order of the

Church," Dimas told him. "I have souls to save in the mining camps."

"Their souls are already gone," Markham said.

Dimas asked him, "Did you attend mass on Easter Sunday?"

"I am not one to argue with the Church," Markham said quickly. "But those are my two best men. You have to know that losing them is a great injustice to me. I demand something in return, as a gesture of restitution."

"What is it you demand?" Dimas asked.

"A dispensation for the remainder of the year."

"So, you want to do whatever you wish, with no threat of sin, until the New Year?"

"You make it sound harsh."

"I will grant you no such dispensation," Dimas told him.

Markham started to light a cigarillo but threw it to the ground instead.

"You should be thankful to me, that I have come for these men," Dimas continued.

"What are you talking about?" Markham asked.

"You don't keep the Holy Days, and you want to sin, with no consequences. So, your restitution, in part, is to allow me these two men. Consider it your duty—a gift to God."

"That doesn't sound right to me."

"That's the way it is. If God chooses to forgive you, that's up to Him. I don't care one way or the other."

"You are a strange priest," Markham said.

Markham stood on the veranda with Bestez, the fog swirling across his domain. He had always complied with any request the Church might make of him, but what would a lone priest riding on a cold morning want with two Indian slaves?

"Saving souls, is he?" Markham pondered.

"Maybe I should go and stop him, to ask and learn more from him," Bestez suggested.

"Why didn't you do that while he was here?" Markham asked.

Bestez shrugged. "You have to be careful with a priest."

"That's just it. We can't have the saints and angels against us," Markham agreed. "To harass a priest is asking for the fires of hell. You know that."

"It is so," Bestez agreed. "But I still do not understand."

"What is there to understand?" Markham said. "At least for now. Perhaps there will be something that will lend us some information."

"You can ask Father Francis," Bestez suggested.

"I will let you ask him," Markham said. "When he

returns, you can learn about this unusual priest who takes Miwoks with him to save souls in the gold camps."

Upon arriving in San Francisco, Maura began to make plans for her venture into building orphanages. She spent some time researching and finally made arrangements to purchase ground on the northern edge of San Francisco. She contracted with an architect to design a building that would serve as both a main orphanage and headquarters for the entire chain. She hoped construction might start in a few months time.

For the time being, Agnes Sterns wouldn't be a part of it. In Sacramento, Agnes had decided she would make arrangements to have a headstone made for her son. She would accompany its delivery to the hilltop above San Andreas, where the politicians had also been interred. Troubled Gulch was no more, except for tattered remnants of a few tents and a quantity of empty liquor bottles lying around. It was no place to bury anyone.

The politician's families had discovered the tragic news in the newspapers fully two days ahead of official notification by the local sheriff's office. The anger ran clear to the governor's office, whose staff members had friends among the deceased. They made arrangements to have the bodies exhumed and brought up to Sacramento.

The violence in the mines had never been real news in San Francisco. But the escalating raids and murders, and the fact that their effects had now reached deep into the political community, would necessarily bring about some sweeping changes—or at least an attempt to bring those changes about. People continued to arrive by land and sea, presenting an ever-growing populace and all the problems that accompanied rapid growth.

Upon reaching the city, Fathers Francis and Manuel had taken the children to one of the Church's facilities, already overrun with the homeless. During one of her visits to see the children she had come to know and love, Father Francis approached her with the idea of taking some of the orphans back to the mines to search for their parents.

"There's a ten-year-old boy and his two sisters who believe they can find their mother," he said. "They know the camp she went to. One or two others will not settle here, either. They would rather go back to the gulches. It might be a way for you to scout locations for orphanages."

Father Manuel agreed to accompany her for a few weeks' time, along with two Franciscan brothers.

"It will provide a measure of safety for you," he

said, "as well as give us an opportunity to see where churches are necessary."

"I'm not quite ready to go back into that atmosphere," Maura said. "Surely, you can understand."

"It's a tough life you've chosen, Miss Walsh," Father Francis said, "with many trials and tribulations."

"I need to prepare myself better for them," Maura told him. "I have a good understanding of what I am about to face and I want to be ready for it."

"I don't believe," Father Francis told her, "that anyone can be fully ready for it."

As Dimas traveled with Cholok and Ramón, he discovered that Percival had certainly given him good information. The two proved to be invaluable as guides. They were young, barely twenty, and sharp-eyed at all times. They knew the country in and around the Sierra Nevada very well and could follow any trail left by man or beast.

Both were skilled at snaring quail and rabbits. They habitually boiled greens and roots and insisted that Dimas eat his fair share.

"Your body needs these foods to fight off disease and fatigue," Cholok explained. "Can you find Joaquín with a high fever?"

Cholok had been named for a special place, called by the Yo Semitee, his people's name for the grizzly bear, where he had been born. His mother had birthed him at the foot of a waterfall. He told Dimas that Cholok meant "the Place Where the Water Falls Down."

The waters there were sacred, and his birth had been viewed by one of the large, powerful bears. Dimas had heard his own father tell stories about them, his encounters with them in the mountains. Their power was beyond description. He had called them silvertips, for their thick and grizzled coats of hair. Cholok considered them his protectors. To have an animal like that present at birth had to mean something special.

Their discussions of bears and the trails north of Miwok home country, the mountains inland to the north, brought Dimas and Cholok closer together. Cholok began to learn that he could speak his mind to this unusual priest without fear of the whip, or being placed in confinement without food or water.

Ramón, on the other hand, was never as trusting. He shunned Dimas completely. Never once could he start any kind of dialogue on any level. It took but a few hours of the first day for Dimas to see that Ramón harbored a great deal of bitterness.

Ramón was small and sickly and, according to Cholok, felt his life had been cursed from the beginning. He had a persistent, consumptive cough, but wanted nothing to do with a white doctor, preferring to wait until he could find a traditional medicine man among his people. He kept making the sign for death, saying that it knew his name and always came looking for him, so Dimas decided not to press it and left him to his fatalistic tendencies.

If Ramón wanted to convey something to Dimas, Cholok spoke in his behalf. Dimas came to believe that Ramón considered him to be bad medicine, a category most of the padres had been placed in over the years. As they rode that fourth night, Dimas came to realize that both of them believed that he had intentionally tricked them into riding to their deaths—that he had personally set up their demise at the hands of the most notorious outlaw in all the gold fields.

"I see you have no more confidence in Percival," Dimas commented to Cholok.

"It isn't Percival we are riding with."

"Do you see Percival as a trickster?" Dimas asked.

"Maybe his reasons for putting us together will show themselves before long."

A day's ride from San Andreas, they stopped in the twilight to water the horses and a pack mule they had acquired along the way. A harsh wind blew across the foothills, and in the near distance an owl hooted loudly.

Ramón dismounted and slipped off by himself to

sing a traditional Miwok song. Cholok kept Dimas a distance away.

"What's he doing?" Dimas asked.

"Singing his death song. He believes his end is very near. We are close to Joaquín."

"Why didn't you tell me?"

"When you trail Joaquín with a stranger, things are done in a certain way," he responded.

"A stranger? I don't understand."

"You didn't tell us everything. You are not a priest. You have worked to make people believe you are, but you're not. But we are bound to you, as Percival sent you to take us from Markham."

"Percival suggested the robes. He couldn't see any other way for me to do it," Dimas explained.

"Why Joaquín Murrieta?" Cholok asked.

"Do you have a brother?"

"At one time, an older one. He was killed in the mines," Cholok replied.

"I still have a younger one," Dimas told him.

"Ah, with Joaquín."

A sudden gust of wind howled. The horses and the mule became nervous and flared their nostrils repeatedly.

Cholok settled his horse and turned to Dimas. "Joaquín. He already knows we're following him."

"When will Ramón be finished with his song?"

"We go no farther tonight, Padre."

"I haven't said we're stopping," Dimas told him.

"Maybe you have eyes like the owl," Cholok stated, "and love the sound of a haunted wind. It's not for Ramón and me."

"Are you afraid to take chances?" Dimas asked.

Cholok grunted. "Just because you're dressed as a Franciscan, do you think Joaquín will spare you?"

"No one, especially an outlaw, wants to die with a priest's blood on his conscience," Dimas replied.

"Joaquín is not the only *bandido* in the foothills," Cholok pointed out. "Joaquín's cousin, Three-Fingered Jack, kills for the pleasure of it. He is a scourge, a plague on the name of Joaquín Murrieta."

They finished watering the horses. Ramón concluded his song and joined Dimas and Cholok. The two Miwoks spoke in their native tongue.

When they had finished, Cholok told Dimas, "We'll keep riding. It doesn't matter where we are now. Death has already found us."

FIFTEEN

As Dimas rode behind his guides through the darkness, the night suddenly became filled with small, whirling twisters called dust devils. Dimas had learned from his mother that the strange twisting winds were wandering spirits, the dead having returned, lost and searching for vengeance.

Cholok and Ramón sang songs and stopped more than once to press pieces of sage into their headbands. Dimas understood what they were doing, and wondered whether the robe might bring him his own protection. As he had promised Percival, he carried no weapons of any kind. For the first time since he could remember in his adult life, he didn't feel the weight of a revolver on his hip.

As he had done often during the trip, Dimas reviewed his plan for meeting with Joaquín Murrieta. As a priest, he would approach the *bandido* leader and try to convince him that injustice was not his cross to bear alone, that many, many others suffered in the same way.

Perhaps in this way he might approach not only Murrieta himself, but his followers, too. There could be no other means by which to sort through the *bandidos* to find Ricardo.

As they neared the top of a hill, Cholok and Ramón stopped to sing a song. Dimas waited for them to finish. They led him to the top of a hill that looked down on a mining camp.

"You had better be ready, Padre," Cholok said. "We have arrived at Hangtown."

Below, a few scattered lanterns flickered among the collection of tents and log and clapboard buildings. Cholok and Ramón stopped their horses.

"We have come to face death," Cholok said. "Let's see if he wants us tonight."

From below came the sounds of gunfire and yelling. It lasted but a few moments.

"Is that what you meant?" Dimas asked. "That little burst?"

"Do you see the sun rising yet, Padre?"

In the center of town, Dimas and his guides discovered a group of people gathered in the street, holding torches and lanterns over two men who lay face down about ten feet apart.

Dimas dismounted and the people parted. He knelt and made the sign of the cross. The two men were both Caucasian, not over twenty years old.

"How did this happen?" he asked.

"Who knows," a miner replied. "They started shooting at each other, like they have been all week long. Tonight their aims were both true. That's the only difference."

Dimas stood up and addressed the crowd. "Are any of you family to them?"

When no one responded, the miner said, "We'll bury them in the morning. I'm getting some sleep."

A young woman, near twenty, with long red hair and snappy blue eyes, stepped forward. "I have two small boys with me at a house at the edge of town. One of the dead men was their father."

Dimas followed the young woman, who introduced herself as Annie Mitchell, to a group of small tents at the edge of the camp. There a number of children of various ages played, talked, or sat and stared out into nowhere.

Cholok and Ramón stood at a distance until Annie invited them in.

"Sit by the fire and have some soup," she said. "There's plenty."

Dimas watched her ladle two bowls full for his

guides. They wouldn't take theirs until she had served Dimas first.

"What do you have here, Annie?" Dimas asked her.

"I've been taking care of children who have no place to go," she replied. "I took in the two boys I told you about three days ago. Their father hasn't been sober for two weeks."

Dimas looked around. "Do you intend to raise these kids alone?"

"Someone will want most of them for their own, sooner or later," she replied. "I lost both my parents to typhus two years ago. I'm just lucky I was older than many of these unfortunate kids."

The children ranged in age from toddler to early teens. They were of many different nationalities, including Chinese, Mexican, Latin-American, and various mixtures in between. A couple of the smaller ones ventured forward and touched Dimas's robe. A toddler touched his face. Dimas held his little hand for a moment and stood up.

"They appear well fed," Dimas observed.

"There are those who contribute to their cause," Annie said.

"That's very commendable," Dimas told her. "It's not all that common, though."

"It isn't," Annie agreed. "But it does happen. A lot

of odd things happen here, like a padre showing up in the middle of the night."

"I have been looking for the *bandido* Joaquín Murrieta for some time," Dimas told her. "I have information that he frequents this area."

"Would you know him if you saw him?" Annie asked. "Or do the papers tell you all you need to know?"

"Outlaws need prayers, too," Dimas told her.

"And outlaws can be answers to prayers," Annie said suddenly.

"Well, you seem to be enacting a miracle of some sort here," Dimas said. "You should have your tents set up at Angel's Camp, not here in Hangtown."

"If everyone was as anxious to take care of one another as they are to find gold, there would be no need for soup kitchens or orphan homes," Annie pointed out.

"You sound like someone else I know," Dimas said.

"Wherever there are children, there's no fear of Joaquín Murrieta," she added. "Let me show you something."

Dimas followed her behind the tents into a log cabin. In the middle of the room sat a crude wooden table, where she said all the kids ate. They bathed, she added, in a large tub in one corner of the room. She moved to the back, along the wall, and shoved a small trunk aside.

"Move closer and hold the lantern, please," she said, kneeling down. "And watch the door for me."

Dimas took a look outside. Cholok and Ramón had joined the children at the fire. Cholok appeared to be telling stories.

Annie called Dimas over, and after brushing some dirt aside on the ground, she opened a buried wooden box. Inside was a large bag filled with gold nuggets.

"You have contributors who give to your church, for your own cause," she said. "We have contributors also."

She told Dimas that the contributions allowed her to pay a muleskinner in gold, once a week, to drop off freight for them. "The kids get good, solid, food and dry, warm bedding to sleep on. That, and a few hugs, is all they ask for."

"You know," Dimas said, "an outlaw can kill one day and do something for penance the next."

"I can say only that the man who is hunted does not harm women and children," she emphasized. "He protects them whenever he can. That's more than I can say for those who chase him."

She told Dimas that the little toddler who had touched his face had lost his mother to illness and that Joaquín and his gang of *bandidos* had brought him to her.

"He risked his life and those of his men to do that,"

she said. "The little boy would have likely died without care."

"Likely he would have," Dimas agreed. "I hope you don't think I am judging him, or anybody."

"Perhaps God is glad for your work," Annie said. "How are you rewarded?"

"My reward is yet to come," Dimas replied.

She looked at Dimas in the lantern light and said, "I've been meaning to tell you this, but it seems so strange. One of Joaquín's men could easily be your brother, you look so much alike."

Dimas stared at her.

"I told you it was odd. You seem a lot like him, in a way. Hard to explain. I'm sorry."

"Don't be sorry," Dimas said. "Do you know this man's name?"

"He often comes with another young man named Chappo," she replied. "Together they bring the gold from Joaquín. I've never asked the second man's name. He keeps more to himself than does Chappo."

"How often do they come here?" Dimas asked.

"It's not regular, just on occasion," she replied. "The one time this man did say something, he told me that he knew what it was like to be without a father, where he grew up near St. Louis. I don't know the place. Do you?"

"Yes," Dimas replied. "I've been there."

"Don't ask me anything more about Chappo or him, or Joaquín Murrieta, please," she said. "You understand?"

Dimas followed her out of the cabin and to the fire. The children were laughing at Cholok's stories.

"We must be going," he said. "Thank you for the meal."

"Where will you go?" Annie asked.

"Back on the trail, to find Joaquín."

"May God be with you," she said.

Dimas nodded. "It's my job to tell you that."

The next morning, Dimas rode out behind Cholok and Ramón. He followed them along trails that wound along steep slopes and through wooded draws, taking a day, then two, riding slowly and deliberately. The two seemed to be in no particular hurry, and though Dimas asked Cholok more than once where they were going, the scout's answer was always "I thought you wanted to meet Joaquín Murrieta."

They arrived on the rim of a deep canyon. The sun rested for a moment at the edge of the horizon and fell below, bathing the steep rocks in purple and gold.

"This is Arroyo de Cantúa," Cholok told Dimas. "As you can see, it's a good place to keep a lot of horses."

"It looks deserted," Dimas remarked.

A group of riders suddenly surrounded them. Dimas hadn't heard them at all, not even the slightest sound.

"No," Cholok told him, "it isn't."

From the darkness came clicks as rifles and pistols were cocked. A man spoke in Spanish.

"Does one of you wear a padre's robes?"

Cholok and Ramón eased their horses behind Dimas.

"I wear the robes of a Franciscan," Dimas replied. "Neither you nor your men have anything to fear from us."

A laugh from the darkness. "Of course we don't."

A large man rode forward. He struck light to a lantern. He wore a red sombrero, lowered over his eyes. Bandoleers crisscrossed his chest.

The moon suddenly appeared from behind fleeting clouds, and he laughed again.

"Are you lost?"

"No. I am right where I want to be," Dimas replied. "Who among you is Joaquín Murrieta?"

The big man rose slightly in his saddle. He turned toward a slim man sitting his horse in the shadows with the others.

The big man turned back to Dimas. "Did you come all this way to hear his confession?"

The *bandidos* all laughed, all except the slim man, who watched Dimas carefully.

"I want to see each man among you," Dimas insisted, "ride past me, in single file, so that I might bless him."

The big man balked. "You give orders in your own place, Padre. This is our place."

"God owns all places," Dimas told him. "Would you dispute that?"

He grunted and rode back to the slim man, who sat calmly. They discussed something and the big man returned to Dimas and studied him, allowing his right hand and the reins to fall across the pommel. Dimas noticed that the thumb and first finger were missing.

"Who should I call you?" Dimas asked him.

"*Séñor* will do," he replied. He handed the lantern to Dimas. "Let me see your face."

Dimas waited for him to comment. He finally asked, "Do you have Yankee blood in your veins?"

Dimas spoke in English. "I must reach people of all cultures."

"I'm not one to argue with a priest," the big man said. He made the sign of the cross over himself.

"Am I wrong to believe you are Manuel Duarte, the one they call Tres Dedos, Three-Fingered Jack?" Dimas asked him. "Cousin to Joaquín Murrieta?"

"How do you know so much about me?" he asked.

"It is my job, as a priest, to learn many things," Dimas replied. "When can I have the men pass in front of me?"

Three-Fingered Jack turned to the slim man, who rode forward. His features were rugged and strong, and flickering lantern light pulled red-blond highlights from neck-length hair that spilled out from under his sombrero.

"I will show my face to you," he said, "since you already know who I am. But my men, each and every one of them, wish to decline your offer, whether or not it comes from God."

Dimas noted that Joaquín's English was not perfect but certainly very accomplished. The same man, Dimas recalled, had stood in the doorway at the inquiry into General Joshua Bean's death in Los Angeles, but was far more intense.

"Why would you wish to study everyone here?" Murrieta asked.

"I want to see if their souls cry out for salvation."

"As a priest, you should be able to tell that from a distance."

"It's the darkness," Dimas told him, "and the wind. You understand."

Joaquín laughed. "Is your soul restless in this wind, Padre?" He turned his horse. "It's a dangerous night. If you and the Miwoks wish to remain safe, you will follow me."

Dimas and his scouts fell in line. In the lead, Joaquín communicated to his men by hand signals, ordering them into a structured formation. He then selected four of them.

"You three must dismount," Joaquín said to Dimas. "For but a few minutes. My apologies, but it is necessary."

The four men, all young but very sure of themselves, proved very adept at handling horses. They calmed them and fitted each one quickly with a form of rawhide boot that slid neatly over the hooves. The boots were tied on securely with thongs.

Dimas was told he and the scouts could return to their saddles. "You can follow or not. It's your choice."

Joaquín left with his men. Dimas waited for them to go down a trail into the lower reaches of the arroyo.

"We aren't going with them?" Cholok asked.

"I'll catch up," Dimas said. "You and Ramón can go wherever you wish. Your debt to me is paid."

Ramón broke his silence toward Dimas. "Will you send us away?"

"You talked about death the entire trip," Dimas replied. "Didn't you?"

"He's saying there's no safer place than with you," Cholok broke in.

"It's true, I thought you would bring harm to Cholok and myself," Ramón said. "Instead, you have brought honor. We found Joaquín and he didn't kill us. Your medicine is much stronger than I thought."

"You are a protected man, it would seem?" Cholok added. "Why would we want to leave you?"

Dimas considered what they had told him. "It's going to get more dangerous from here on."

"More so for you," Ramón remarked. "You are a *pistolero* without pistols. Is it possible for you to remain that way, even wearing the robe of a Franciscan?"

Dimas didn't answer. It was Cholok who said, "He will remain true to his mission. If he touches a pistol now, he will never make happen what he wants."

Dimas rode behind the scouts as they trailed Joaquín and his band. Cholok and Ramón kept looking behind.

"Joaquín's back scout is too noisy," Cholok remarked. "I hope he can hear any danger before it hears him first."

They camped at the head of an arroyo filled with trees. Everyone bedded down in the open, and with first light Joaquín awakened Dimas by putting a tin cup of coffee under his nose.

Dimas rose and thanked Joaquín for the coffee.

Near a small fire, he announced to Joaquín, "I need to hear confessions soon."

"Why should a *bandido* confess what he is about to do over and over without remorse?"

Dimas noted that all of Joaquín's men were already actively sharpening knives and loading revolver cylinders with powder and ball.

"They don't want to confess?" Dimas asked. "Surely all your men don't feel that way."

"Should they decide to leave me, take up something else, then you might be right," Joaquin acknowledged. "But until that happens, why should they confess anything?"

"How do they do penance?"

"There's a hill not far away. My people climb it on their knees to see Our Lady at the top. Many of my men have been there. That's enough."

Dimas struggled to figure a way to get a look at Joaquín's men, to locate Ricardo among them.

"Perhaps you are a God to your followers," Dimas said, "but you can't make God's decisions for Him."

Joaquín grunted. "Perhaps not, but as I told you, I can make their decisions for them as long as they follow me."

"They have a right to discuss their wrongs and their sufferings, if that's what they wish," Dimas argued.

"Tell me about suffering, Padre." He stripped off his shirt and exposed his back. Whip scars crisscrossed it from his shoulders to his hips. "My wife, Rosa, has suffered even greater than this. She sits day after day, rocking back and forth. Some days she doesn't know me at all."

"I'll pray for her."

"How can your prayers help now, Padre? They came to our claim on the Stanislaus River. They said my brother, Jesús, stole one of their horses. So they hanged him and then took turns with Rosa, holding me back. They said that I should live to remember what had happened, to take the memory back to Mexico with me. I will always remember, but I will not go back to Mexico until I'm finished with my business here."

"Do you think killing Anglos will make things better?" Dimas asked.

"Ah! You see! You assume that I want to kill all of them. Not so. There are far too many to ever accomplish anything that way. To me, it is more important to take away what is most important to them. Their wealth. There are many *peones Anglos* as well. It is the rich who have found a means by which to take everything from the people. So I find the ones who have the most, and I take their gold and their horses, but I don't kill them. Then they are shamed and have to live with that. Isn't that worse than death?"

"Perhaps you have a plan in mind, but you are being branded a murderer in the papers," Dimas pointed out.

"I can't be everywhere at once, Padre," Joaquín told him. "But I can be where I want to be, leading my men, and I can take what I want, whenever I want."

"I should still speak to your men," Dimas insisted.

"They don't have to listen to a priest," Joaquín told him. "Your church has caused great suffering and has taken a great deal also."

"Did I ask you for money?"

"My men are more important to me. I don't want them worried about what they are doing because you decided to scare them."

"If you never intended for me to do my duty, then why did you have me camp with you?" Dimas asked.

Joaquín pointed to where a large man walked toward them from the trees.

"It is important that my cousin, Tres Dedos, and I part ways," he told Dimas. "I want you to bless the meeting."

"Why should I be a part of it?"

"If you are truly concerned about death and dying, you will listen to me," Joaquín insisted. "Tres Dedos rides with me and camps separately with the men who believe in him, in defiance of me. He rides away without notice and raids where and when he pleases, then comes back and brings bad fortune. He believes those who follow me will soon turn to him, because he believes himself to be the better leader."

"Why don't you let it prove itself out on its own?"

"I already have. For reasons you will soon learn, it's time for this meeting, and I want him to know that the Church sanctions it."

SIXTEEN

Tres Dedos joined Dimas and Joaquín beside the fire. He had been eating beans and tortillas and dried beef. He swallowed a mouthful of food with coffee.

Dimas made the sign of the cross. "The peace of Christ be with you both."

Duarte stared first at Dimas and then at Joaquín. "You have taken the padre on your side in this matter?"

"You heard him say he was on the side of Christ," Joaquín responded. "Whatever comes of this is for the best."

"Padre or no, and Jesús or no, this will not be a pleasant meeting, Cousin," Duarte said. "So maybe we should get right into it."

"As you wish," Joaquín agreed. "How many of the men see it your way?"

"All of them."

"Ah, then if you ride away now, they will all follow?" Joaquín smiled. "Yes, some of them will. But those who do will forfeit their gold first."

Duarte's eyes blazed. "Do you want bloodshed within the family?"

"It is the rule, Manuel. I am leader, and our raids took place under my command. Whoever goes with you can have what they take at another time under your sole command."

"Your rules are trite and silly, Cousin."

"They are still rules, something you have no use for. I have asked you not to make so much trouble that doesn't need to be made, to kill so much when the killing isn't necessary. Now the highest law in the land comes for me with no quarter, when it was you who couldn't leave the fandango alone without bloodshed."

"It wasn't just me, Joaquín. Many others wanted the same thing," Duarte insisted.

"Perhaps, but you could have said, 'No, this should not happen. We have more important business than this.' But you didn't. Now the governor and the men at the state capital have decided to show me that I am not fit to live any longer."

"Who stole Markham's horses and killed Markham's men?" Duarte responded.

"Are the politicians in Sacramento crying over Markham's men? Or their friends who were dragged through the mud at Troubled Gulch?"

Duarte threw his cup aside. Coffee splattered and the cup clinked off the rocks.

"I will become even more famous than you, El Famoso. You'll see. Then you'll wish you had me by your side when the Yankee gringos come to take your head."

Tres Dedos stomped back to the other camp. He saddled his horse, which signaled those who sided with his cause to follow suit. A few within Joaquín's group gathered their things to join them. They left any gold or stolen valuables in a pile.

Dimas accompanied Joaquín while he walked among them. He struggled to locate his brother. He saw no one who even looked remotely like Ricardo.

"Be certain of your choice," Joaquín cautioned them. "If you leave with Tres Dedos, you will remain with him. That's how it must be."

Dimas continued his search, but to no avail.

Arguing, yelling, and fistfights broke out among the men. Some of those who wanted to leave with Duarte quarreled with those who wanted them to remain with Joaquín.

Dimas started toward the other camp, where Duarte's men were getting ready to leave. Three-Fingered Jack stopped him.

"Where do you think you're going?" he asked.

"Perhaps some of your followers want to confess."

"You don't hear any confessions today, Padre. Your prayers are too weak for my blood."

When Duarte and those who had chosen to ride with him were gone, Dimas called his guides to him.

"I will be ready to leave in just a short while," he told them.

Dimas waited while Joaquín gave his men orders to get ready to depart.

Dimas approached the outlaw leader.

"I have to ask you, is there a man named Ricardo among your men?"

"Three of them."

"Ricardo Dimas?"

"There is one Ricardo Dimas. Is he a very important soul to you?"

"Yes, but each one is important."

"Of course they are," Joaquín agreed. "But the next time you are asked to pray before an important meeting, make certain you say the right prayers."

Dimas rode behind his guides, contemplating how he might make his way back and find Ricardo. When they stopped to water the horses, Dimas told them, "This time we can part company. You've done more for me than I could have possibly asked. I think it's best."

"You don't always know what's best," Cholok

responded. "Don't go anywhere for a few days. Come to my people's camp and rest and think on it."

"A few days and Ricardo could be dead."

"If you go to Joaquín, sneaking around to look for your brother, you will be dead."

"Listen to Cholok," Ramón put in. "Don't do anything foolish. What good would that do your brother?"

Dimas followed behind them, high into the foothills, on into a beautiful area filled with high rock outcrops and waterfalls. Cholok told him his people called themselves Yo Semitee and that the name had become familiar to the miners in the area.

As they arrived, a group of laughing children ran out to greet them, followed by a half-dozen young men, who hailed Cholok and Ramón warmly.

They were ushered into the village and seated in a place of honor. Soon Dimas was stuffed with a stew filled with quail and roots and selections of elk and deer as well.

Cholok and Ramón sat with group of male elders. Though they conversed in their native tongue, Dimas noticed readily that they were speaking about him and his daring approach to Joaquín Murrieta. None of it made any sense. He had failed to complete his mission.

Frustration took hold, and for the next few days, Dimas remained off by himself. The people respected his wishes and left him to view his troubles in his own way. Finally, on the third day, Cholok approached him.

"Are you getting some vision of what you must do?" he asked.

"I'll go back to Hangtown and wait for Ricardo to show up with this other man, Chappo," Dimas informed him.

"Do you know for certain when they will return?" Cholok asked. "How long can you be there waiting before the people begin to wonder about you?"

"So what do you suggest?"

"There's food and shelter here for as long as you wish to stay," he replied. "Until you have a vision of what you must do."

"I don't know how to do that," Dimas confessed. "I just sit and worry."

"This area is sacred," Cholok told him. "If you go into the Yo Semitee and listen to the ancients, something will come to you."

"I'm not connected to this area. I have no ancients here."

"Everyone is connected everywhere," Cholok explained. "That's how it works."

By late May Maura had gotten her finances in place for the orphanages and felt ready to begin her quest to establish them in the gulches. She had thought about it seriously and had decided to eventually return to Los Angeles and pursue the joint effort with Elisa to turn her boardinghouse into a safe place for orphans. That would come after getting things underway in the camps.

Father Francis had already returned to Los Angeles with an escort of clergy and parishioners from Sacramento and San Francisco. Their intention was to bolster the diocese there and make inroads for Maura and Elisa.

Father Manuel had remained behind. He and two Franciscan brothers would escort Maura through the camps, providing a measure of safety and confidence, though they realized she had enough gumption of her own. She would never set out on her own, anyway, and welcomed their help.

Her first destination was a camp named Placerville, better known in the foothills as Hangtown. The afternoon of their arrival, a party of vigilantes had just lynched five Mexican miners. Shouts and arguments filled the air, then quieted with the presence of Maura and the priest and two brothers.

"Who is responsible for this?" Father Manuel asked. When no one stepped forward, he added, "Is there none among you who would take credit for this brand of justice?"

At that point a man separated himself from the others. His left arm was missing.

"I was with the group, but I don't favor hanging a man just on hearsay. I hope God will forgive me."

"Where are the rest of the vigilantes?" Father Manuel asked.

"Gone to the next gulch, to look for Joaquín Murrieta," another man said.

Father Manuel stood beneath the dangling bodies. "So, who are the men that were hanged?" Again, no one answered. "Certainly not Joaquín. How did it come to pass that these men died and Joaquín is still on the loose?"

"They were thought to be men who rode with him," the one-armed man said. "That one on the end, he confessed to it."

Maura pointed out the whip marks, now welts filled with dried blood, that had aided in their interrogation.

"He's whipped until he confesses," she suggested, "because after a time he believes death to be a relief."

Father Manuel turned to the crowd. "Is that how it happened?"

Everyone began to disperse. Maura stopped them.

"Did any of these men have families?" she asked.

"Go find Annie Mitchell, at the far end of town," the one-armed man said. "She takes care of orphans hereabouts."

Maura located the string of tents with ease. Annie Mitchell introduced herself and, upon seeing Father Manuel, commented, "This must be a stopping spot for Franciscan priests."

"Father Francis must have passed through," Father Manuel ventured.

"Why would he come north?" Maura asked.

"True," Father Manuel acknowledged.

"He was a strong man with strong features," Annie said. "He never told me his name. I mentioned to him that he looked like someone else who sometimes comes here, as if they might be brothers. He got a funny look on his face. That's what I remember most about him."

"You say he was a priest?" Maura asked.

She pointed to Father Manuel. "The very same robes."

"I can't imagine who that would be," Father Manuel said.

Annie studied Maura. "Are you all right?" she asked.

"There's just one surprise after another on this trip," she replied. "Where did the priest go?"

"He left with his scouts, but he'll be back, I know that," Annie replied. "I could see it in his face."

Maura told Annie about her plans for setting up a string of orphanages throughout the gold camps, in both the northern and southern mines. Annie grew excited at the prospect of becoming a part of the plan.

"Tell me," Maura asked, "how have you been able to afford to feed and clothe these kids?"

Annie was evasive. "Contributions from individuals."

"Enough to cover everything?"

"So far," Annie replied. "Now you've come along and there's no worry about that any longer."

"It looks like you've already gotten things well started here," Maura observed. "I'll do what I can to improve things for you."

They were interrupted by the sounds of gunfire. A group of riders entered town, shooting their pistols into the air, led by a large bearded Anglo man with long, wild hair and eyes to match. He led the men straight through to the boardinghouse and dismounted.

He took two five-gallon cans from two of the men and set them on the ground. Maura and the others stood up.

Father Manuel stepped forward.

"You, priest, needn't interfere with this," the big man said.

Father Manuel leaned toward him. "I beg your pardon."

The big man pushed past him. "I'm looking for a

little lady named Annie," he said. His eyes narrowed. "Would you be her?"

Annie took a step back. Maura asked, "What is the nature of the visit, sir?"

"The nature of the visit, ma'am, is in regard to Joaquín Murrieta," he replied. "I'm sworn to find him, by legal writ, granted by the governor of the state of California." He opened his topcoat, U.S. Army, captain's issue, to reveal a metal star. He also pulled a paper. "I'm the head of the newly and properly organized California Rangers."

A crowd began to gather, but remained a distance back. Maura studied the big man and the rest of the rangers with him. Aside from the army uniform vests and tops, she found it difficult to distinguish them from any of the groups of common ruffians that frequented the mining camps.

"My sources say that the killer Joaquín has come to this town and these particular tents more than once," the big man continued.

Annie had trouble speaking. "I don't know the man, sir. Really."

"Perhaps there's been a mistake," Maura suggested.

"I don't make mistakes, ma'am," he said. "I came to do my job as I see it."

"Do you see an outlaw gang here, sir?" Maura asked.

The big man looked into two of the tents.

"I don't believe the children carry guns," Maura told him.

"I'll be on my way," the big man said. "But I'll have men watching this place. Be sure of it."

The big ranger handed the cans of alcohol back up to the riders. He mounted his horse and led them out of town.

The one-armed miner approached Maura. "There was another priest who came through here not long ago," he said. "Wisht he was here now. He'd have stood up to that big bastard."

"No one seems to know his name," Maura remarked. "Didn't anyone ask him?"

"You're certain he was a priest?" Father Manuel asked.

"Are you a priest?" the one-armed man responded.

"Of course," Father Manuel told him.

"I figure, since he was dressed like you, he would have answered the same. But like I said, that bastard who was just here would have gotten an earful from him."

"I don't understand what's going on here," Maura put in. "That man said he was a ranger. Dressed in an army overcoat?"

"Guess you haven't heard, eh?" the one-armed man

told her. "That man was Harry Love, given full office to bring Joaquín Murrieta in any way he sees fit. Those cans of alcohol they had with them? For pickling. Word is, the reward will be granted for Joaquín's head."

SEVENTEEN

Don Luis Markham decided that a number of things had suddenly threatened his ability to keep his ranch. He still steamed at the fact that the politicians had been killed. It made no difference who had actually killed them; Joaquín Murrieta had been blamed. That meant his best source of cover had literally been placed on the chopping block.

Though the point was moot, he lamented the fact that he hadn't gone north with the herd himself. He had expected too much from Bestez, who had been in charge of Sterns as well as the vaqueros and the horse herd. It had all been too much and believing Sterns to be able to make strong decisions had been a mistake. That mistake now threatened his ranch.

He worked to digest the facts that had forced him to make new decisions. He had ordered Bestez, along with a select group of his vaqueros, to get ready to leave with him for the mining camps. The rest would remain to keep the operations going.

As the men brought their mounts and packhorses to the main house, Bestez dismounted and joined Markham on the veranda.

"You think this is best, Don Luis?" he asked.

"I see no way around it. Do you?"

"It all depends on where Joaquín is right now," Bestez replied. "He could be anywhere on the Vereda del Monte. He could be north, or he could be well on his way to Mexico. Nobody knows."

"You can be sure that this Harry Love fellow is close to him," Markham said. "A man like that has a nose like a dog."

"If we kill this man, Love, how can we be certain everyone will think it was Joaquín who did it?"

"Who else will they believe did it? Who else is Harry Love chasing?"

"This is much different than raiding the tables for gold," Bestez pointed out.

"Are you afraid to do it?" Markham asked.

"Not afraid, just cautious."

"What we must concentrate on," Markham said, "is to keep Joaquín Murrieta alive and well. We cannot allow his death or capture. Should that happen, our raids would come to an end. Can you see that?"

"But perhaps there's another way that must be considered," Bestez suggested. "The flow of gold is less and less. Soon there will be so little to take as to render it impossible to make the payoffs. Then what?"

"There will never be too little to take," Markham insisted. "You can't think that way."

"But we have to look at what is real, Don Luis."

"Listen to me! I'll tell you what is real, do you understand?"

Bestez stepped back. "But of course."

"Nothing is going to change. Nothing at all," Markham emphasized. "Everything is going to remain the same around here. I will see to it."

"Yes, you will."

"But you don't agree, Bestez. You just said so. You just told me to accept something different."

"I don't want to fall out of favor, Don Luis," Bestez pleaded.

"You will have to do something very important then," Markham responded. "Something that will surprise and please me greatly. Do you understand?"

"But of course." Bestez waited for Markham to settle down. "The truth is, it won't be so easy to find Joaquín, I don't think."

"If you believe what Father Francis told you, then it will become very easy, won't it?"

"I suppose it will, providing the *pistolero* can find his brother."

"And you're sure that Father Francis talked to the *pistolero* in person?"

"Father Francis talked to him before going north. The *pistolero* was sitting at the boardinghouse with his legs shot. He must have bled a lot but didn't die. We should be able to find a strange priest with two Miwok guides easy enough."

Markham lit a cigarillo. "If John Dimas can lead us to Joaquín, where his brother is, then if we stay close, you can be sure that Harry Love will be there at some time or another."

"Most assuredly," Bestez agreed. "When we get Love, is it finished?"

"What do you think? Who came here and made a fool of me? Who will surely try and have the authorities here wondering about me? Who do you suppose would like to take everything away from me? Who can do us more harm, really, than if Harry Love catches Joaquín Murrieta?"

"I believe you want John Dimas worse than you want this Harry Love fellow," Bestez said.

Dimas hadn't settled in at the Miwok camp. He acknowledged the hospitality but never spent a moment in peace. Cholok and Ramón rode out one morning and returned with the news that Joaquín and one or more of his bands had taken a herd of mustangs to Mexico. It seemed certain, according to their sources, that the *bandido* leader would return, but no one could say just when.

As Dimas's frustration mounted, the people made every effort to make him feel welcome and to keep plenty of food in front of him. Cholok's mother, a small woman named Angelica who had greeted her son with long hugs and tears upon their arrival, spoke fluent Spanish, and some broken English. She insisted that Dimas accept a gift of deerskin moccasins from her, for bringing her son and Ramón back to the village.

"I was certain he'd been killed," she said. "I will always owe you much more than this for returning him."

"I'm not the only one to thank for it," Dimas told her. "There's someone who knows them pretty well, it would seem."

Angelica smiled. "Yes," she said, "I know who you mean. You haven't seen him for a time, I do know that."

"I'm not going about this right," Dimas lamented.

"So far it hasn't been wrong. I know you're not a priest, and it's not bad to dress like one. I believe you've been true to the vows, though."

"I don't know about any of it," Dimas admitted. "So far it hasn't done much for me."

"You're still alive, and you haven't discovered that your brother is dead. That's worth a great deal."

"I may never know for sure," Dimas told her, "either way."

"Still, you have to be able to live at the same time, to be yourself and let it go."

"You don't understand," Dimas insisted. "The longer I wait to go look for him again, the more likely I'll never find him."

"But if you go to the wrong place, then what?" she pointed out.

Dimas had to admit she had a point. Still, it continued to eat at him. Angelica discussed the situation with him daily, assuring him that when he was to go to a given place, he would know.

One evening she approached him in camp.

"I think that maybe your luck has just changed," she told him. "There's an old man down by the creek. I believe you've been waiting for him." She pointed. "Go down beyond where the women are filling their water bags."

"He's here? How do you know him?"

"We all know him," she replied. "He comes here and stays for a time. You had better go before it gets dark."

Dimas took the trail down the hill. He passed women and children, talking and laughing among themselves. He reached the creek and hurried past more women and children. He soon began to wonder if he had heard Angelica wrong.

He reached a large, split-trunked black oak, just up from the creek, where a small burro stood tied to one of the limbs.

"I thought you would never get here," said Percival from the shadows under the tree.

Dimas started toward him. "She didn't say I'd have to walk until nightfall."

"You should know by now that this time of day is my favorite," he said with a laugh. "I like to watch the sun lower itself. The coming night is ready to breed a new mixture of things to come. I like to be in between, to see how the two relate."

"It's hard to follow you, Percival."

"Take a seat on the hillside."

Dimas didn't sit down, but began to pace instead. "I wasn't allowed to see Ricardo. He didn't trust me."

"Do you blame him?" Percival asked. "After all, you're no priest. You're alive only because he respected your nerve, your brash behavior."

"Why didn't he say something, then?" Dimas asked.

"He let you do most of the talking; or no talking to speak of, in the case of blessing the meeting with Three-Fingered Jack. A real padre, especially a Franciscan, would have had everyone say at least one rosary."

Dimas stared at him. "You met with Joaquín? He told you all this?"

"There are others who were there, too, or don't you remember?"

"I asked about Joaquín. Is that the only answer you're going to give me?" Dimas pushed.

"It's enough," Percival insisted. "No matter, you were there and it didn't work the way you wanted it to. Now you need to decide what's next."

"Maybe the robes weren't such a good idea after all," Dimas said.

"How would you have done it? How many pistols can you fire at one time?"

Dimas began to pace again. "Who wore these robes before me?"

"What does it matter?"

"I think I'm feeling something that person felt. Is that possible, that these robes carry some kind of memories, or something? From the shooting?"

"Maybe it's coming from you and has nothing to do with the robes." He studied Dimas. "Why do you think your feelings and sensations are different than anyone else's, whether or not they wear a Franciscan robe or a gambler's dark suit?"

"This robe has a hole from a .44 ball in it."

"You've taken rounds from pistols yourself. I see

you don't walk so well yet. And you've shot balls into people. Maybe the feeling, when you really look at it, isn't so much different?"

Dimas considered his comment. He studied the old man, as well as it was possible to study him, hidden in the shadows.

"I don't how to proceed," Dimas lamented. "Harry Love is bound to find Joaquín sooner or later. I don't want Ricardo with them when that happens."

"That stands to reason," Percival agreed. "There's a high hill not far from here." He pointed north. "You'll know it because there will always be a few people at the top, praying. Go there and climb the hill on your knees."

"On my knees?"

"Joaquín told you about that hill, too, didn't he? That makes two of us telling you to do penance."

"My legs are still sore, Percival."

"All the better. A Franciscan does those things."

Dimas struggled to understand. "What will I see at the top?"

"Tell me when you see it."

"You are getting more mysterious all the time," Dimas told him.

"That's because you're seeing things a little better all the time. But your eyes aren't completely open yet."

"What is it you want me to see?"

"Find yourself a mirror and look into it."

"My job is to find my brother, Percival, you know that."

"You will never find your brother, John Dimas, until you find yourself."

Dimas turned to walk back to the village. "Aren't you going to meet with the man Cholok's mother told you about?" He pointed downstream. "Just a short ways from here."

Percival rose and untied his burro. He began to walk away.

"I don't understand," Dimas called after him.

Without a word, Percival disappeared into the shadows. Dimas turned and walked around a bend in the stream. He noticed a small campfire, where an older man sat roasting a rabbit.

Dimas approached cautiously. The man had once been large in stature but now appeared frail and tired. He looked up at him.

"Hungry, Padre?"

Dimas recognized the voice instantly.

"Father, is that you?" he asked.

The man stared at Dimas. "John? My son, John?" His breath escaped him. He held out his hand. "By all that's holy in this world, where did you come from? And a priest?"

Dimas shook his father's hand. It felt strange. He

should know this man so well, but in some ways he seemed more distant than any stranger he'd ever met.

"I'm wearing these robes to find Ricardo," Dimas explained. "Mother passed last year. Before she died, I told her I would come out here and find him."

His father sat quiet, gazing into the fire. He held out a cut of meat. "Better have some rabbit."

Dimas accepted it with thanks. "I know you never approved of Ricardo's behavior."

"Maybe that's how you saw it from your angle," he suggested.

Dimas thought about it. "I was a child, true, and perhaps saw things from that perspective. You didn't really let anyone know."

"Maybe he and I had some conversations you weren't privy to."

"Could be. Do you know where he is now?"

"Do you?"

"He's with Joaquín Murrieta. He wrote letters to Mother. I'm going to get him to quit before it's too late."

"So you figure the priest garb will gain you an advantage?"

"So far not. But eventually."

"No matter if you do get to talk to him, you'll have a hard time getting Ricardo to turn about," his father said. "Guess I'm to blame for most all of it."

"I've always wondered. Why did you have to go back to the mountains?" Dimas asked.

"Even if I could have handled a sedentary life, it didn't seem like I had anything left there," he replied.

"Didn't Mother always welcome you back? It seemed like it."

"She made it look good for you and Ricardo. We had our differences, and they grew with the years. But that wasn't the most of it." He chewed hard on his piece of meat. "When I came back the second time, Ricardo avoided me entirely, and you wouldn't let yourself get that close to me. I don't suppose I can blame you for it. You were sure I'd leave again and didn't want to go through all that."

"I'm sorry, Father. I never meant to hurt you."

"I'm the one who did the hurting, John. You and Ricardo both. Pretty deep, I suppose."

Dimas leaned over, and his father opened his arms. The two hugged each other, allowing years of grief to pour out.

"I looked for you all over the mountains," Dimas said.

"I left the cold climates some years back." He laughed. "The sun works wonders if your bones are as brittle as mine."

"When I find Ricardo, I'll bring him here to see you. Mother would like that."

"John, there's something you should know. She wasn't your real mother. Your mother died when you were born."

Dimas recovered and asked, "Why didn't anyone tell me?"

"She was Ricardo's mother. Your mother was one of these people here. Spanish and Miwok. You were born behind the waterfall, like some of the others."

"But why didn't I know?"

"For what reason? You called her Mother and for all practical purposes, she didn't treat you any differently, did she?"

"I suppose I thought she did at times."

"Favorites are favorites. Mothers are mothers. Among these people, a baby belongs to at least ten women, not just the one who bore the child. It makes no difference. But there are still favorites. Ricardo fell into that category."

"I don't know if I can manage to make contact with him or not," Dimas said.

"Maybe you're not meant to. Ever think of that?"

"I made a promise."

"I'm sure you've learned by now that you don't have full say over everything."

"I'm beginning to get the picture."

"Time to let it go, then."

Dimas stiffened. "I don't know if I can do that. Not until I know for sure where he's at."

"Suit yourself. Maybe you've already fulfilled your promise to the best of your ability. But that's for you to decide." He cut another piece of rabbit and divided it. "I was for leaving you in the village here for the women to raise. But Cholok's mother, Angelica, said, 'No, there is a woman who needs him for her son.' One of the other women nursed you for a couple of months, while I trapped the Colorado River. Then I came back for you, and within a few days I met the woman who was to become Ricardo's mother, your new mother."

"It doesn't matter now," Dimas acknowledged.

"I'm not a wise man, son," his father said. "It's just that I've learned some things about life. I know a person, wherever he comes from, has to make his own way, how he sees fit, and keep his eyes open for help along the way. Sometimes you learn things you didn't expect to, and that can mean reviewing your next move in life."

"I have some things to review, I'll acknowledge that," Dimas told his father. "I'm going to find Ricardo and bring him here so we can catch up on things."

"I wish you luck, son. I surely do."

EIGHTEEN

Maura watched with enthusiasm as the builders broke ground for the new orphanage. It wasn't meant to be an overpowering structure, just big enough to accommodate thirty to forty children at a time. Her plan was to then work with Annie to move them to San Francisco or down to Los Angeles.

After everything was established and rolling smoothly in Placerville, Maura intended to see what might be accomplished in San Andreas and then go on down to Los Angeles and reconnect with Elisa. The more she thought about it, the more she believed the young woman would be a good partner in her plans.

Father Manuel and the two brothers busied themselves with counseling and other regular duties, but became anxious to move on, especially at the news that Joaquín Murrieta had returned from Mexico and might be in the area. They wanted no part of the blood that could come when Harry Love and his rangers finally located El Famoso and his gang.

Maura hoped the building construction might progress well and rapidly but harbored a secret hope that it might go on just long enough for her to possibly see John Dimas. Based on descriptions Annie Mitchell had given her of the mysterious padre who had arrived a while back with two Indian scouts, she was certain it had to be him.

She realized, though, that she couldn't count on it and worked to keep from getting her hopes up. It had been some time since she'd last seen him, but she felt they had visited in thoughts and dreams. She felt it had to be more than just fantasy, for the resultant feelings were far too strong.

In their short and sporadic times together, they had made a connection. That much she knew. He had kind eyes that reflected pain and, often, an anger that had built over time. Yet when he looked at her, she felt something she had never felt before. She knew he saw her as special, somehow, and would love to be with her as much as possible.

She had grown to want the same thing. How that could be possible, she couldn't understand. It was a desire from within that she had to acknowledge as something far different than any experience she had ever known. As the time passed, her memory of him had grown stronger, not weaker. Whatever it was, she felt compelled to pursue it, if even remotely possible.

The Hill of Our Lady proved easy to find. Dimas arrived early in the morning to give himself enough time to climb to the summit on his knees and not be pressed by darkness. Percival had told him that some of the people took two days to get there. He didn't have that kind of time.

He began, holding his robes up to keep from falling forward. Rocks ground into his knees. A rain came and went. He persisted, all the while noticing people walking back down from the summit. They stared and pointed, and some touched him, crying.

By noon his vision had blurred slightly, and his legs were cramped. His mostly healed gunshot wounds throbbed and sent spikes of pain up and down his legs.

Shortly thereafter he felt his strength waning. A woman stopped and looked into his eyes.

"Draw from within," she instructed. "Your strength will return when you begin to do penance in the name of those who have wronged you."

This confused him. Do penance in the name of those who had wronged him? He stared at her, and she answered his question.

"You must do the penance for those who agreed to become the instrument of your pain. They cared about you enough to do those things, so that you might learn."

She was gone, but Dimas still questioned that he had heard her right. Perhaps, when his mind cleared, he would better understand.

A ways further he leaned over onto his hands and knees and breathed deeply. The air held no sustenance. The top seemed too far to reach. He started to rise to his feet when he heard a voice in his head.

"You were always the strongest, the bravest. You always withstood every test, whether it was physical or mental."

Dimas held his breath. His mother's voice. His father had been right: she would always be his mother.

"It's not as far now as you think. You can make it."

Dimas felt his eyes dampen. "Where's Ricardo?" he asked. No response. He repeated his question. It was as if he had imagined the voice.

A slight wind touched his face. A woman passed him on her knees, her shawl close about her face, working her way toward the top.

Dimas remained on his knees and started after the woman, straining to keep pace. His knees and legs began to grow numb, and he fell forward twice, then a third time as he neared the top. The woman ahead of him disappeared over the summit. When Dimas arrived, he stood up, fell down, and regained his feet. He steadied himself and saw no one.

He turned a circle, and another. No one else was there. A few women with their children stood a ways downslope, staring at him through the distance. They turned and eased themselves down the hill.

He turned around, but there was still no one else around.

"Where did you go?" Dimas asked into the wind.

"Here."

Dimas turned. The voice came from no particular direction, more a feeling than a sound. He listened and heard only the wind.

He viewed an altar made of slab rock that held candles and earrings and lockets and bracelets and other forms of jewelry, plus some strips of colored cloth. A large figurine of the Blessed Virgin presided over the offerings. Mashed blueberries and wild hyacinth had been used to paint her hands and face, and her robes.

Confused, Dimas asked, "Why do you have my mother's voice?"

"A mother is a mother to all," he heard in his mind and body. "Why are you really here? Do you really care to find your brother?"

Through the intense pain, Dimas felt his anger rising.

"Why would I come all this way otherwise?" He heard nothing. "Why did you send me here to do this?" he continued. "You were always making me take care of him, when he never wanted it and never listened to me. And why did you take your anger against my father out on me?"

He stared at the figure, but still heard nothing. He turned again and viewed the sky and the lower hills and the people, now farther down the slope.

A wave of emotion passed through him, and was carried away on the breeze. Then another.

He saw his mother, lying on her deathbed, her eyes nearly faded. She looked to him, and he suddenly knew that her reason for asking him to find Ricardo had nothing to do with his brother.

"You can save yourself, if not him," he heard her say. "If you truly want to. You can be someone different."

Pain welled up from deep within him.

"When you find Ricardo, listen to him carefully," she said, and faded away.

He turned his face to the sky. The wind now grew stronger and began to fill with a steady rain.

Markham led his men into San Andreas with Bestez at his side. The news that Joaquín Murrieta was in the area had reached every camp. The streams were no longer filled with prospectors angling for position.

Markham took note and sent word ahead that he was willing to compensate the man who could give him the information he wanted. Wherever they had stopped along the way, the talk was of new depredations against miners, travelers, and dealers in the gambling halls. The papers gave equal time to the big, wild-eyed ranger and his deputies, who turned camps upside down looking for El Famoso.

San Andreas shared the anxiety. In a rundown saloon filled with miners with nothing to do but talk and worry, Markham was approached by a one-armed man.

"I hear you're offering money for some news," he began.

"For the right news, yes," Markham replied.

"Well, I don't know that much about Joaquín, but if I heard it right, you're wondering plenty about that Harry Love fellow that was here a while back."

"What do you know about him?"

"There's some miners here set to become rangers," the one-armed man continued. "Word is Love has a lead on Joaquín's whereabouts and will come through to pick the men up."

"I'll pay you to know what day that is," Markham said.

"That don't seem quite fair," the one-armed man complained. "How am I to know the exact day? Information given should be information paid for."

"Tell you what," Markham said. "Maybe you can learn from some of your friends when Love will be here." He flipped him two gold pieces. "I'll double that if you bring me something solid."

"I'll bring you something solid all right," the one-armed man promised. "You can count on that."

Dimas rode from the Hill of Our Lady toward Hangtown, staying to the back trails that Cholok and Ramón had shown him. They had more than performed their duty. They had brought him right where he wanted to be, and he couldn't ask for any more than that.

He knew also that they would always be grateful for his delivering them from Don Luis Markham and for giving them an opportunity for renewed life with their families. At least the robes had done that much since he donned them.

He hadn't seen Percival since the night he found his father. He had a lot of questions, but as he well knew, there was no predicting when or where the old man might appear.

He arrived in Hangtown in late evening. Most people now referred to the growing camp as Placerville, but Dimas could never see the place as that civilized. He would give his mission a final try, and, success or not, he would leave it to rest.

The camp resounded with its usual activity, but at the edge of town, along the creek, it was quiet.

Annie was cooking for the children over an open fire. He dismounted and she approached him.

"She's been expecting you."

Dimas turned. "Maura?"

"Good to see you, John. Padre John, I should say."

"What a nice surprise," he told her. "What did I tell you about goodbyes?"

She smiled. "You're a prophet as well, it would seem."

Annie returned to feeding the children. Dimas and Maura walked along the edge of the creek.

"I'm sorry about Trenton Sterns," he told her.

"I had a bad feeling about his going with the politicians, but he insisted. I hope he's at peace."

"I thought you were staying in San Francisco," Dimas said.

"I've decided to go forward with my plans. Your reputation precedes you. When did you become a Franciscan?"

"I'm not officially ordained."

She smiled. "Your robes aren't a bad fit."

"Believe me, they are."

"Have you located your brother yet?" she asked.

"I found Joaquín, but wasn't allowed access to his men," Dimas replied. "Annie told me that a young *bandido* named Chappo delivers gold dust here for Annie's children. She said Ricardo is often with him. As I see it, it's my best bet."

"You've already done a great deal to find him," she said.

He pulled the gold piece from a pocket and held it up. "I'll get the rest of it done. Your little gift won't fail me."

Maura smiled. "I have to admit, John, I've been thinking about you a lot, too. I worried about you being killed."

"Markham's men almost got it done. Shot me in both legs." Dimas studied the gold piece. "I spent some time recuperating in a pretty spot called Puddingstone, a little ways from Los Angeles. Soft breezes and waterfalls. I'll show it to you some time."

"That would be nice," she said. "Sounds like a good place to take orphaned kids on an outing."

"Give them some good memories to carry with them," Dimas agreed. "It's a good thing you're doing, Maura."

"I don't just want to house and feed and clothe

them," she told him. "I want them to learn how to break out of their plight and go upward in life."

"How did you do it?" Dimas asked.

"I decided to make the best of where I was at the time, but I know that I could some day make a much better place for myself in life."

"That's admirable," Dimas told her. "You certainly have proven that to be true."

"I believe anyone can, if they decide to," she said. "It allowed me to understand the concept of sowing good seeds to produce good fruit."

"That's one of my lines, you know."

Maura smiled. "I suppose you've gotten pretty used to your role now."

"These robes taught me some things, that's true," he said. "But their time has just about passed."

"What will you do then, do you know?"

"Could you use help getting the orphanages going?"

She smiled. "I can always use help with that. As a matter of fact, I'm going with Father Manuel and the two brothers down to San Andreas tomorrow. I want to assess the need for an orphanage there before I go on down to Los Angeles."

"You're going to work with Elisa, then?"

"She'll be very good," Maura replied. "If you find Ricardo, you're invited down to help."

"I'm looking forward to it," Dimas told her.

Maura tugged lightly at his robe. "Do you intend to make this permanent."

Dimas pulled her close. "Like I said, I don't fit the mold."

Their lips lingered together and Dimas led her farther along the creek and into a secluded spot.

Dimas slid her dress down over her shoulders. His lips trailed along her neck.

Maura helped him out of the robe. "I've always wondered what you wore under this," she said with a smile.

NINETEEN

As the sun fell, Dimas strolled beside the creek, out from town, immersed in his thoughts. Maura occupied his mind as much or more than did Ricardo. Three days had passed with no sign of his brother. Three days since he had last talked to her, and still he felt she was with him.

He perceived a conflict and tried to discern what was to be kept and what was to be let go. His time on the Hill of Our Lady suggested to him that he didn't have the means to answer it, to just go forward with his plans to find Ricardo, at least for a little while longer.

He turned around to start the walk back to Hangtown when he saw a burro tied beside the creek. An older man stood in the shallows poking through a gold pan.

"Damned if there ain't a few nuggets here in these

gravels," Percival said. "Looked all that time before, and now I stumble onto it. Ha!"

"Rich is rich, no matter your age," Dimas commented.

"Now you're getting the idea," Percival responded. "Maybe your quest is over at that."

"How do you mean?"

"I say, you made the climb to Our Lady and you saw your old Pa. That's a lot to do in a short time."

"I did learn that even if I don't see Ricardo, I know better than to consider him more outlaw than me," Dimas confessed. "There's a lot of things that I could be taken to task for myself. I was a Texas Ranger and like these rangers who are after Joaquín, some of the things I chose to do in the name of the law were questionable."

"So you have changed," Percival observed. "Maybe now you know not to shoot people first and ask questions later. That there's no one who needs killing. Maybe you'll see your pistols as a last resort from now on, not a first response."

"I believe it's time to permanently remove the robes," Dimas said.

"Oh, not so fast," Percival said. He pointed toward a rider who had just arrived and was talking to Annie near a campfire.

"Who's that?" Dimas asked.

"Go see," Percival replied.

Dimas left him and approached a young vaquero wearing heavy chaps and a sombrero low over his face. Dimas knew that without the robes, the young man would have either run the other way or tried to shoot him.

"Oh, you're the priest who came to our camp," the young vaquero realized. "Who is not a priest. Strange."

Annie offered an introduction. "This is Chappo."

"I believe you're good friends with my brother, aren't you?" Dimas asked. "Ricardo Dimas?"

A figure emerged from the shadows, leading a strong black mustang. He stood a couple inches shorter than Dimas but weighed nearly the same.

He ventured close to the fire and handed his mustang's reins to Chappo.

"You and Annie can water the horses if you'd like."

"Ricardo," Dimas said. "My brother."

Ricardo kept his distance. "The way Joaquín described you, I knew it could be no one else. What a fool."

"A fool, to come to find you? How long has it been?"

"I haven't kept track," Ricardo replied. "Have you?"

"Sometimes I think about it, yes. What happened between us?"

"You need to ask? Have you no memory of the past?"

"It must be different than yours," Dimas suggested. "What do you hold against me?"

"I was going to ask you that," Ricardo responded. He kicked a stray coal back into the fire. "You always saw me as a bad one. So I decided to grant your request. How's that?"

"I saw you as never wanting to be happy, never wanting to keep out of trouble, that's all."

"Is it up to you to make me happy, Brother? Or anyone else, for that matter?"

"Mother passed. Before she died, she asked me to find you."

"You saw the letters?"

"It matters that she asked me, Ricardo."

"And you were certain of success, weren't you?" He began to pace. "You always felt you had to take everything on your own shoulders. You should learn to leave things alone sometimes."

"Don't you understand, Ricardo? I came here to save your life. I promised our mother that I would grant her dying wish."

"It's a noble thing you did, Brother. Now you can rest easy."

"How about our mother?"

"How can we know how she rests? That has nothing to do with all this."

Dimas restrained himself from going toward his brother.

"How long, Ricardo, have you been without a soul?"

"Think about it, John. What there is between you and me, it's beyond her now. It's completely up to us, and always was just between us. She's gone, and what happens here, in this place, does not matter to her any longer."

"Why do you show such disrespect?"

"On the contrary," Ricardo insisted. "You shouldn't hang on to her and have her concerned about the outcome here. Don't you see that people cannot pass on easily if there are family members clinging to them?"

"I told you, it was her idea," Dimas responded.

"Fine. Now let it go."

"I have to tell you, I'm not surprised at your response."

"At least you've learned something."

Dimas took a moment. He recalled the voice he'd heard at the top of the hill, and the thoughts their mother had left with him before fading away, about listening to what Ricardo had to say. Perhaps he was right. Maybe they would have had a much better relationship had he kept from preaching to his brother.

"It's true, I have learned something," Dimas agreed. "A few days back I learned a lot from Our Lady."

"You climbed the hill on your knees, to the top, to the shrine?"

"Yes," Dimas replied. "You should do it some time."

Ricardo extended his hands toward the firelight. "I made the crucifixion walk this Easter."

Dimas stared at the holes at the base of both his brother's hands. As a common Easter penance, men would offer to be crucified. Not until death, but until they felt they had completed their penance.

"Do you remember as a child, when we were at an old cabin and you pierced your hand with a nail?" Dimas asked.

"No," Ricardo replied. "I don't remember that."

"I told you not to, but you did it anyway?"

"Are you sure?"

"I don't know why you'd forget that," Dimas said. "What made you do the Easter sacrifice?"

"Like you, it seemed like our mother wished it," he replied. "I thought I heard her talking to me."

"You could have died."

"I wanted to. They took me down. It's time to go."

Ricardo started away and Dimas stopped him.

"Please, Ricardo. Leave Joaquín."

"I'm not with Joaquín. I'm with Three-Fingered Jack."

"That's worse."

"You're still at it, eh, Brother," Ricardo pointed out.

"Ride away with me, Ricardo. Leave this all behind."

"And do what? Even if I wanted to, where would we go?"

"We could work for someone on a ranch. There's need for vaqueros and managers. Always."

"I tried that way once, Brother. Never again." He motioned to where Chappo and Annie stood a distance away with the horses. "I wasn't getting paid, so I paid myself. A very fine horse, eh?"

"Whose is it?"

"I just told you. Mine."

"Whose was it before?"

"Don Luis Markham misses him greatly, I'm certain." He noted his brother's expression. "You know Don Luis Markham?"

"Only too well."

"I was going to join my friend, Chappo, and raid for Markham, but he whipped Chappo for no good reason," Ricardo explained. "So we stole some horses and left in the dark."

Chappo and Annie returned. "We had better get back, Ricardo," Chappo said.

Ricardo dismissed him. "In a minute."

"You don't have to go back, you know," Dimas told his brother.

"Do you want to hear this or not?" Ricardo began to pace again. "Shortly after we left Markham, I set up a raid for Joaquín, through an old hombre named Percival. We took a lot of Markham's horses into Mexico. Joaquín took me into his band. We came back up here, and that's when I wrote the letters."

"I was in Los Angeles when Markham's men struck and blamed it on Joaquín."

Chappo stepped back over and leaned toward Ricardo. "He's the one I told you about. The *pistolero*."

"Oh!" Ricardo said, "you're the one who shot Markham's men to pieces? They say you killed fifteen of them."

"The numbers grow."

"Still, good shooting."

"I don't want it to catch up with me," Dimas said. "Not any more. I'm taking a different trail."

"I'm glad to hear it. Now, as Chappo said, we're late in getting back."

"How long has it been since you've seen Father?"

Ricardo turned. "I can hardly remember what he looks like."

"He's in the Yo Semitee village. Let's go and see him together."

"Maybe, after we take the horses we have down to Mexico. Maybe not. Maybe I won't return. I haven't decided yet."

"You know that Harry Love and the rangers are looking for Joaquín and Tres Dedos," Dimas pointed out. "How long do you think you can hide from them?"

"Chappo and I have decided to go down to Mexico with another one of the Joaquíns," Ricardo announced. "Joaquín Murrieta and Tres Dedos are meeting at Cantúa to take the other half of the mustangs to Mexico together. Perhaps they want to have another meeting and patch things up, I don't know. I just want to run horses."

"I know Cantúa," Dimas said. "I wish you'd see Father with me first."

"Something to think about," Ricardo agreed. He mounted his black mustang.

"After we see Father," Dimas added, "we could ride on down to Los Angeles and you could see Carlotta."

Ricardo grunted. "What don't you know about me? Where do you plan to go?"

"To Los Angeles, through San Andreas. I met a woman, too, who I'd like to get to know a lot better."

"That's good, Brother. We'll see where the trails lead." He turned his horse and led Chappo off into the darkness.

Annie stood with Dimas as they left. "I worry about them both," she said.

"It's too late for worry," Dimas told her. "Maybe too late for prayer."

"Before you go," she said, "an old man left some things for you. Buckskin clothes, a large knife, and two pistols."

"An old man left them?"

"He had a burro with him. He said the burro was hard to get along with."

The one-armed man watched while another stranger rode into town. San Andreas brimmed with newcomers. The man looked to be a *pistolero,* but somehow his face seemed familiar.

He approached the stranger and asked, "You come to join the rangers? If you have, you're too late."

"I don't care to join them at all," Dimas told him, looking down from the saddle. "I ran into them a ways back and they detained me for two days."

The one-armed man grunted. "I'd say you look dangerous."

"I'm looking for a woman named Maura Walsh," Dimas continued. "She's supposed to be starting an orphanage here."

The one-armed man stared at the dark brown robe tied over the back of Dimas's saddle.

"A right pretty woman?" he asked Dimas. "Traveling with a priest and two brothers?"

"That's her. Do you know where I can find them?"

"Didn't you used to be a priest, yourself?"

"The woman and the clergymen. Where did you say they went?"

"I'd look a couple of miles up the road, at Troubled Gulch," the one-armed man replied. "Nothing there anymore, deserted, but I was standing nearby when three men said she needed to go get some orphans over that way."

"Three men?"

"They rode in a while back with that Californio from down Los Angeles way. Markham was his name. He pays in gold for the right information."

"Markham is over in Troubled Gulch?"

"No, I told him some good information. He went off toward Cantúa Canyon, after Harry Love, and left his right-hand man here. His name's Bestez. I get paid to listen well."

"What about Bestez?" Dimas asked.

"Markham left him to find out about someone named Dimas. John Dimas. You know him?"

"I believe I do," Dimas replied. He turned his horse. "I'll be going now."

The one-armed man squinted even harder, and yelled after him. "You did, too, used to be a priest."

Dimas found Troubled Gulch completely deserted except for ten horses tied outside a clapboard saloon. Dimas dismounted and took the robe off the saddle and strolled inside.

Bestez and his men turned. They had bottles lined up in front of them. Maura sat off to one side at a table still filled with cards the poker players had left behind on their way out.

Father Manuel sat beside her, along with one of the brothers. The other one lay dead on the floor.

Dimas walked over and tossed the robe onto the table.

"You can't face all of them," Father Manuel warned Dimas under his breath.

"Yes, he can," Maura said.

Dimas moved away from the table and faced Bestez.

Bestez's mouth dropped. "What? Ah!" he yelled. He turned from the bar. "John Dimas! The *pistolero!*"

"Too bad your knee never healed, eh?" Dimas said.

The men with him scrambled over tables and chairs to go out the back. Bestez placed twitching fingers on the butt of his revolver.

"Go with them, Bestez," Dimas warned him.

"I'm not ready to leave," Bestez growled.

"Shooting clergymen is bad luck," Dimas told him.

"He wouldn't stay seated," Bestez explained. "He wasn't a priest, just a brother."

"Well, no matter," Dimas said. "You still have time to catch up with your men."

"Why do you have to spoil it?" Bestez whined. His fingers twitched harder. "I promised Don Luis I would do something special for him." He motioned toward Maura. "Look who I found."

"Can't you understand, Bestez? Your welcome here is over."

"I have no place to go."

"Find Markham and tell him his time is over, like you said."

"I have other choices. I have lots of gold. You and I, we can make a deal for the lady."

"No deals, Bestez. It's over."

"You know, I told Don Markham this wasn't good. We should just find another way to keep his ranch."

"He should have listened to you. Now you can ride away and go where you want. You don't have to go back to him."

"What about my honor, Señor Dimas? What would I have left of my honor?"

Bestez reached for his pistols. Dimas pulled and

fired. Bestez reeled back into the wall and over a nearby monte table and groaned before lying still and silent.

Father Manuel and the brother went over to Bestez's body. The priest began to pray.

Maura sat for a moment at the table. Dimas helped her up.

"You've changed, John," she said. "It really bothered you to have to do that."

"Did they harm you?" he asked.

"They never so much as touched me," she replied. "I was supposed to be a present for Markham."

Everyone turned to the saloon door as it filled with the presence of a small one-armed miner.

"You put those fellows on the run, I'd say," the one-armed man said to Dimas. "Guess Bestez played the fool."

"You looking for information?" Dimas asked.

"Came with some," he replied. "If you hadn't left in such a hurry I could have told you back at San Andreas. You have a brother named Ricardo?"

"What about him?"

"He rode in yesterday looking for a certain priest. Said he was this priest's brother and wanted him to know he had decided to listen to him, that he wanted to talk to their father. That he'd meet him at Cantúa and take him up on going to Los Angeles."

"I don't have any gold," Dimas said. "But a lot of thanks."

"You'd better go, *pistolero,* and let me and the clergymen do the burying," he said. "Word just came in that Harry Love just reached Cantúa."

TWENTY

Dimas and Maura rode throughout the night. They reached Cantúa as day broke, with haze hanging low over the canyon floor and out into the valley far below.

"It seems deserted up here," Maura said.

"That's deceptive," Dimas told her. "Listen, I think I hear horses."

They rode a short distance farther and stopped where a number of horses stood, including the black mustang that Ricardo had been riding.

Dimas and Maura stiffened at the sound of pistols being cocked.

"I came to meet my brother, Ricardo," Dimas said quickly, his hands in the air.

Joaquín Murrieta and members of his gang emerged from cover.

"So you are no longer a priest, eh?" Joaquín said. "You can both step down from your horses."

Dimas dismounted. "You could never allow an imposter to discuss matters of faith with your men, could you?" he said. "I should have realized it then, that you saw me for who I was."

"I had never seen it done before," Joaquín said. "I was curious. You were more sincere than some priests I've met, though."

"Once again," Dimas said, "I've come for Ricardo. This time at his request."

"He's camped down below, with Tres Dedos," Joaquín said, "where the creek comes out of the canyon."

"But this is his black mustang."

"No longer," Joaquín told him.

One of Joaquín's men stepped forward. "Ricardo is a good man, but he doesn't play poker well."

From below came the sounds of gunshots, rapid and from many different pistols. Without another word, Joaquín and his men mounted and were gone.

Dimas and Maura quickly climbed on their horses.

"What's happening?" Maura asked.

"My guess is Harry Love found the lower camp. God help Ricardo, and all of them."

Dimas and Maura rode a ways farther, and before they could react, Don Luis Markham and his men had surrounded them.

"An interesting morning already, wouldn't you say, Señor Dimas, the *pistolero?*"

Markham instructed two of his men to step forward. Dimas was relieved of his knife and pistols, and his hands were then tied behind him.

"Tie the woman, too," Markham ordered. "She can be a feisty one."

Markham led the way to the top of the canyon and sat his horse at the rim. The sun had risen and the haze had lifted. A few gunshots continued to ring out from below, amid columns of swirling dust.

"It's good to know that Joaquín wasn't down there," Markham said to the group. "Whoever was there must surely be dead."

"Bestez told me something," Dimas ventured. "He said your day was past. He was right. Even if Joaquín lives, your ways are gone forever."

"Bestez never understood how things truly are," Markham said. "He never looked at it in the right manner. Now, you see, with the rangers and the *bandidos* occupied with their fight, they've left a lot of horses for me to take. I am the true victor, and I will collect the spoils for myself."

When Markham had instructed a number of his men to locate the loose mustangs, Dimas asked, "What do you want with us?"

"The woman has always been mine," he replied. "I just took my time in claiming her. As for you, there has to be justification for Bestez's death. Doesn't that seem fair?"

"You talk as if I were a commodity," Maura told him. "You had smoother words on your rancho, when I wasn't tied up."

"Ah, but that is the point," Markham acknowledged. "A strong filly needs to be bound well to be broken right. I've always said that."

"You're not much of a *mestenero*," Dimas challenged him. "A good one doesn't need to use force."

Markham rode up to Dimas and struck him across the face with his quirt.

"You try my patience, John Dimas."

"And you prove my point," Dimas told him. "There's no reason we should be bound. You have all your men around you, and you've taken my knife and pistols. What are you afraid of?"

Markham motioned to one of his men, who rode up behind Dimas and cut the bonds loose.

Dimas rubbed his wrists. "I appreciate that."

"Your turn to accommodate me," Markham responded. "Remove your buckskin shirt."

Dimas sat tight on his horse. "I'm comfortable the way I am."

"You don't do things fairly, do you?"

"I recall the last time I was without a shirt."

"Maybe you should dismount then," Markham said. He got off his own horse. "See, it's not so hard."

Dimas remained mounted. Markham motioned to one of his men, who quickly threw a noose over Dimas's shoulders, took a turn of the rope around the saddle horn, and jerked him backward.

Dimas hit the ground hard. He struggled for breath.

Markham approached and hissed, "Who do you think you are, *pistolero?*"

He struck Dimas across the back of the head with his quirt. Dimas sagged forward, and Markham began to kick him savagely.

Dimas tried to rise, but Markham's boots slammed the wind from him and left him gasping.

"What is wrong with you?" Maura yelled.

Markham laughed. "See, his buckskin shirt comes off easily now." He threw the shirt aside and pulled Dimas's head up by the hair. "He seems to be a little dazed. That's good."

Markham began to work on Dimas's legs, first with the quirt and then his boots, kicking and pounding him until he had to stop and catch his breath.

"It's hard work, doing this to you," he told Dimas.

The men who had left suddenly rode up and announced that the hills at the head of the canyon were covered with grazing horses.

"All of you, go get them and take them out through the canyon," Markham ordered. "I'll join you very soon."

One of the men grabbed the reins to Maura's horse.

"No," Markham told him. "Leave her here."

Markham's vaqueros departed. Maura sat tied to her horse.

"What do you intend to do with us?" she asked Markham.

"I already said, you are going to be mine from now on," Markham replied. "But first I want you to see something."

Markham led her horse over to where Dimas struggled to rise to his feet. He tied her horse's reins to a tree near the edge of the canyon, where she could clearly see over the top.

"You should have a wonderful view from here," he told her.

She struggled to keep her balance in the saddle as the horse jerked and pulled at the reins, nervous at the proximity to the canyon rim.

Dimas had come to his hands and knees. Markham approached from behind and kicked him down.

Working quickly, Markham took the noose from

around Dimas's shoulders and tightened it around his neck. He laughed as Dimas struggled to breathe and looked over at Maura.

"It's time for a hanging."

Her horse continued to prance nervously. From the far end of the canyon came the sound of hundreds of running horses. A cloud of dust began to develop.

"Yes, and my men will soon be here," Markham observed.

Maura worked to keep her balance on the jittery horse.

She slipped one leg over the saddle and balanced herself with her bound hands. The frightened horse turned one way, then another.

Markham continued to peer up the canyon to where the herd of horses thundered toward them. Dimas grabbed him around both ankles and pulled hard. Markham fell backward to the ground.

With what strength he had left, Dimas slammed a fist into the rancher's face. The two men fought until Dimas couldn't find enough energy to continue.

Markham rose to his feet. After kicking Dimas hard in the ribs, he laughed.

"You aren't getting out of this," he said.

Again he kicked Dimas, over and over, knocking the wind from him. He grabbed the rope and dragged Dimas toward the edge of the canyon. Dimas struggled to keep from choking, working to loosen the noose around his neck as Markham pulled him along.

Below, the horses and the vaqueros driving them grew ever closer.

Maura took the chance and jumped from the saddle. She rolled away from the edge as the terrified horse snapped the reins and bolted away into the trees.

At the rim, Markham tied the rope off around a tree. He pushed Dimas onto his stomach and pulled both wrists behind him. Dust boiled up from below as the horse herd began to pass by.

He started to tie Dimas's wrists together when he felt Maura's foot slam into his back. Dazed, he lurched up and turned. She kicked again. He laughed and grabbed her leg and pushed her to the ground, landing on top of her.

"Wait," he said to her. "I have to do something first."

He hurried to the edge of the canyon. Dimas had come to one knee. Markham grabbed him under the arms and hoisted him to the rim of the canyon. Frantic, Dimas grabbed a leg, but Markham stripped his hand loose and pushed him over the edge.

Dimas felt himself falling, bouncing off the steep slope. From directly below came the sound of hundreds of hooves hammering the canyon floor. He reached up and grabbed the rope just above his head and pulled with all his might, to keep the noose from snapping his neck. He held tight as he came to a jolting stop.

Dangling precariously, he managed to stabilize his swinging motion and began to hoist himself back up toward the top as dust and noise boiled up from below.

Maura, her hands tied behind her back, struggled to her feet. Markham grabbed her from behind and turned her around.

"You'll get used to me," he told her. "You'll be glad to have a man like me."

Maura turned her face away as he tried to kiss her. She brought a knee up into his groin, and he grunted in pain. Still, he grasped her tight and wrestled her to the ground.

Dimas pulled himself up over the edge. He removed the noose and gasped for breath as he struggled to his feet.

Maura saw him and couldn't help herself. "John! Thank God!"

Markham turned and pushed off Maura. He charged Dimas, who sidestepped him and struck a heavy blow to the side of his head. Markham staggered and Dimas pounded his midsection, and then his face.

Again Markham lurched, grabbing one of Dimas's arms. The two men struggled and stumbled to the ground at the canyon's edge. Dimas slipped on the loose rock, feeling himself sliding closer to the edge with Markham.

They slid to the rim and partially over. With all his might, Dimas slammed a fist into Markham's elbow. The joint popped and Markham released his grip.

Dimas gripped a rock outcrop and hoisted himself free of Markham's desperate attempts to grab his legs.

The loose rock under Markham gave way. He grabbed a small tree in desperation as his legs and stomach slid into space. Dimas leaned toward him, but the seedling began to rip loose.

Markham's eyes grew wide. He said to Dimas, "Do penance for me," and slid backward, screaming, down, down, into the dust and pounding hooves below.

Dimas caught his breath and Maura helped him up. After recovering to a degree, they caught their horses and were met by El Famoso.

"So, it is no more for Don Luis Markham," he commented. Shooting started again from down below. "It was nice of his men to drive the horses through the canyon for us," he added. "Now my men will relieve them of their burden."

"The earlier shooting?" Dimas asked. "Was Ricardo there?"

"Harry Love and his rangers surprised a number of the men camped at the mouth of the canyon," Joaquín replied. "Ricardo was lucky enough to be out catching his horse at the time. They killed maybe a dozen, took two heads. One of them belonged to Tres Dedos. They took his hand as well."

"The other head?" Dimas asked.

"Ricardo's friend, Chappo."

"How could they think he was you?" Maura asked Joaquín.

He shrugged. "They needed to have somebody. There's a lot of money to be paid. When we went down to bury the dead, we learned that Chappo told them he was the leader. The rangers started shooting. Ricardo is still down there, mourning his friend."

"So they have killed you?" Dimas asked Joaquín.

"For a while," Joaquín said with a grin. "My men and I will take the horses to Mexico. Then I'll see what I want to do."

With that, he disappeared into the trees.

A night breeze flowed off the Sierra Nevada. The small fire felt good to Maura and Dimas. Ricardo could not be comforted.

"We have come a distance from where he died," Ricardo said, "but he will always remain close to me."

They had discovered Ricardo at the edge of a bank that had been collapsed. The bodies of the slain lay under it, the soil trampled over by horses.

"It was the best way to leave them," Ricardo said. "No one can disturb them now, ever again."

"Los Angeles will be a new start," Dimas promised. "You can have a good life with Carlotta."

"I believe you're right, Brother," Ricardo replied. "I'm willing to try it."

Dawn found them eating dried beef and cold beans. "The food is better down there, too," Dimas said.

Unusual for summer, a fog covered the valley, and by midmorning, the visibility still remained poor. They prepared themselves to depart. Maura pointed to a small burro that wandered out of the haze and stood with its halter dragging.

"Is that the burro you talked about?" she asked Dimas. "That belongs to the old man you know so well?"

Dimas replied, "It's the same burro."

He led the burro around, but there was no sign of Percival.

"The way you always talked about the man, he always seemed kind of mysterious," Maura commented.

"He is that, but interesting as well, as I also said. And as good a friend as I've ever known."

"Where is this man?" Maura asked.

"Hard to say," Dimas replied. "We'll just take care of this little guy, I guess."

"Why would his burro be here and not him?" Ricardo asked.

"You would have to know Percival to understand that," Dimas replied. "Let's go on to Los Angeles."

AFTERWORD

John Dimas and his brother, Ricardo, are characters of my imagination, as are most all of the others in the novel. However, the celebrated Mexican *bandido* Joaquín Murrieta, the inspiration for Zorro, did indeed live and have a history in the violent gold fields of 1850s California.

The legends surrounding Murrieta's life are conflicting, but there seems little doubt the impetus for his insurgence began with the reported violation of his wife, Rosa, and the death of his brother, Jesús, by hanging, at the hands of a group of miners over an alleged thievery of a horse or mule. Joaquín himself suffered a severe whipping.

The incident exemplified the conditions that existed in the mining camps following the Mexican-American War and the subsequent Foreign Miners Tax, imposed at $20 per month on all but Anglo prospectors.

The history of the California gold fields is complex

at best, and represents the hopes and dreams of a large contingent of people willing to risk everything in their quest to better their lives. This included Chicano, Latino, and Chinese families, as well as representatives of nearly every European nationality that had immigrated to the United States, as well as many who arrived from the Old Country directly, to enter the creeks and streams of the Sierra Nevada foothills.

How Joaquín Murrieta chose to react to his own personal indignation, and that of his family, set the stage for a violent and revolutionary period in early California history. Reports of depredations committed by Murrieta and one or more of his gangs made front-page news for more than two years.

On May 11, 1853, California governor John Bigler signed legislation authorizing Captain Harry Love, a onetime Arizona Ranger, to organize a similar group to be called the California Rangers. According to the wording of the decree, they were to disassemble or disband by any means possible a "party or gang of robbers commanded by the five Joaquíns." These men were listed as Joaquín Botellier, Joaquín Carrillo, Joaquín Murieta (sic), Joaquín Ocomorenia, and Joaquín Valenzuela. This labeled the listed men and their followers as responsible for most of the rustling, robberies, and murders perpetrated in the mining camps during the previous three years.

A reward of $1,000, plus expenses at $150 per month for each man, was offered for proof of the *bandido*'s capture and removal from California society.

In July 1853 Love and a group of his rangers attacked a camp of *mesteneros* at a location known as Arroyo de Cantúa. Accounts vary, even among those purported to have been there at the time. Documented, however, is the fact that two heads and a deformed hand were taken. One of the heads, considered to be that of Tres Dedos—Three-Fingered Jack—was soon discarded by the rangers. Damage from gunshot wounds had caused a rapid deterioration. The other head became famous throughout the saloons and museums of the Mother Lode country.

THE HEAD

of the renowed bandit

JOAQUÍN!

AND THE

HAND OF THREE-FINGERED JACK!

THE NOTORIOUS ROBBER AND MURDERER.

Debates raged as the head and hand, preserved in jars of alcohol, made the rounds. More than a few people believed that Harry Love had collected a bounty for the wrong man. He also collected some $5,000 additional, after the initial thousand, from the state coffers as a bonus. This remains a mystery no one seems to have ever solved.

Genealogical records document the fact that Joaquín Murrieta was known for his reddish-blond hair, as were two of his cousins.

An Alta California editor spoke out in print:

"It affords some amusement to our citizens to read the various accounts of the capture and decapitation of 'the notorious Joaquín Murieta [*sic*].' The humbug is so transparent that it is surprising any sensible person can be imposed upon by the statements of the affair which have appeared in the prints. A few weeks ago a party of native Californians and Sonorians started for the Tulare Valley for the expressed and avowed purpose of running mustangs. Three of the party have returned and report that they were attacked by a party of Americans, and that the balance of their party, four in number, had been killed; that Joaquín Valenzuela, one of them, was killed as he was endeavoring to escape, and that his head was cut off by his captors and held as a trophy. It is too well know that Joaquín Murieta [*sic*] was not the person killed by Captain Harry Love's party at the Panoche Pass. The head recently exhibited in Stockton bears no resemblance to that individual, and this positively asserted by those who have seen the real Murieta and the spurious head."

The following year, John Rollin Ridge, who wrote under the pen name Yellow Bird, published *The Life and Adventures of Joaquín Murieta* [*sic*], *the Celebrated California Bandit*, a fictionalized account of the events leading up to and following the attack by the Anglo miners.

Harry Love continued to exhibit the head and hand at the rate of $1 per person until public interest dwindled. At that time, an investor from San Francisco invested in the exhibition with the intention of taking it across the United States. The head and hand were reportedly on display at the Pacific Museum and were permanently lost in the 1906 California earthquake.

The true facts are most certainly lost within the layers of legend and drama retold over the years. What remains is an interesting view of early California during the height of gold fever and of a man who became a legend in the cause of equality among men of all races and creeds.